Dr. Bones
═══ AND THE ═══
Time Machine

BY
Charles Shamey

Mosaic Design
Book Publishers

DR. BONES
AND THE
TIME MACHINE

First Printing – May 2017

ISBN: 978-0-9968933-5-0 *(paperback)*

Printed in the United States of America on acid-free paper.

Published by Mosaic Design Book Publishers
Dearborn, Michigan USA

0 1 2 3 4 5 6 7 8 9

DEDICATION

This story about happy kids is dedicated to another group of happy kids — my children and grandchildren.

To the memory of Niemer and Winona, you helped to make my childhood so wonderful.

Mr. DeKay Helped to make Salina School " A Time to Remember." Charles ☺

Acknowledgements

I wish to thank my daughter, Alicia Shamey Haidar, for taking time to serve as editor of this delightful story about a group of kids who grew up in a cosmopolitan neighborhood who remained lifelong friends and always "true to their school."

I also thank Pat O'Hara, whose father taught at Salina School, and gave permission to use the pictures during the sunset dance.

Thanks to the fine people at the Dearborn Historical Museum for protecting the legacy and memory of the Salina parade that helped bring to life through photos the fabulous parade you will read about.

Thanks to Joe Borajo and Rudy Constantine for inviting me to help preserve the precious history of our beloved Salina School.

The original Salina School, two floors and two rooms, opened in January of 1918.

DR. BONES AND
THE TIME MACHINE

There is a wonderful saying that holds true for all the school kids in America, "Be true to your school." The kids who have attended Salina School, nestled in the neighborhood of the Henry Ford Rouge Plant, began believing this in 1918. It was January that year when the very first Salina School opened its doors, and the massive bell rang out from the belfry on the first day of school. It replaced the Rouge School that for decades served the community. Mr. Henry Ford bought several hundred acres of land and began plans for building the greatest and largest factory in the world, closed the Rouge School, and helped to open the new Salina School on Mulkey Avenue which later was to be renamed Wyoming Avenue. It wasn't long before ground was broken to build a bigger school to house the many children that would move to the neighborhood as their dads found employment at the Ford Rouge Plant.

Henry Ford was building the Eagle submarine chaser to be used to chase German subs during World War One. The most popular tractor in the nation and Europe, the Fordson Tractor, was being built at the new Rouge Plant, too, so people from many parts of the world began moving to the neighborhood to work there and their kids would attend Salina. As the factory grew, so did the population. By 1921, so many kids arrived to attend Salina that the community began building a bigger school with three floors.

Salina School completed in 1926. The center was finished in 1922 and in 1926 new wings were added for hundreds more Salina students.

Many famous people were to be associated with and attend Salina in those early days. The family of Joe Penner, a great American comedian and movie star from the 1920's and 1930's, lived right on Salina Street. In 1932, at the height of his fame, he came and performed his comedy routines and made everyone laugh when he quipped, "Wanta' buy a duck, yuck, yuck." Adele Mara went to Salina and was a well known Hollywood movie star. One of her famous films was with John Wayne in the "Sands of Iwo Jima." David Seldon was a teacher there before World War Two and after joining the service, he came home to stay in New York. He became the president of the American Federation of Teachers. It is rumored that Johnny Weissmuller, Tarzan in the movies, swam in the school's pool. He was a friend of a Salina kid who grew up to be an African big game hunter. Another famous person who found his way to the neighborhood was America's greatest athlete, Jim

Thorpe. In the 1940's, he took a job with Ford as a security guard and often came to the neighborhood for lunch. He would play football and buy treats for the teens. Whether famous or not, rich or poor, or what religion or ethnicity, the kids from Salina were devoted to each other and loyal to the present day. Through the decades, people would remark how the Salina kids stuck together. Through thick and thin, right and wrong, they stuck together. The American way!

This story, about seven kids from Salina School, happened in 1955. The school was the focal point of the lives of all the kids in the neighborhood. Rock and Roll was alive and well and the songs and dancing were part of their lives, too. The kids had lots of places to hang out. Among them was, Tripepi's, a family run store. It was located next to the school were the kids would hang, eat, dance, listen to the juke box — six plays for a quarter, and play different arcade type games. Sophie, the owner, would bring in these games from arcade companies. The juke box was next to the baseball pinball machine which was next to the one booth in the store. She had a long counter with stools, a grill, candy showcase, and she served delicious hotdogs and chili for lunch. The store was portioned down the middle and on the other side were groceries, bread, vegetables, lunch meats, and lots of other market items. Customers came in and put their purchase on the "bill" which meant it was marked in a book specific for each family. The "bill" was always paid on Friday — payday. Dads got paid!

The gang was comprised of Phil, Charles, Neemer, Alan, Robert, Pat, and Lynn. They remained lifelong friends. Let's go back to 1955 and look in on the gang.

"Hey guys, here comes Mother Simpkins," hollered Phil.

"Ooh!" the boys rang out in unison while they were sitting on the school bars.

Mother Simpkins made her daily walk to Tripepi's store each day from her home. She was beautiful. She reminded the gang of the movie star, Ava Gardner. The gang couldn't take their eyes off of her — because she was so beautiful. One of the gang would help her carry the bags of groceries home. The gang grew up around Salina School in the South End of Dearborn, Michigan. They would often meet and sit on the school bars. The bars formed the perimeter of the school lawn so that students would not cut across the grass.

The gang spent a great deal of time at the corner of Salina and Lowrey. In elementary school, they manned each of the four corners as safety boys crossing the little children each morning, noon, and after school. In junior high, they became the leaders of the safety patrol, which had more than forty members, became outstanding athletes, and champs in basketball. In one basketball game, they scored 104 points and made the front page of the local paper. There were some really busy streets in this neighborhood and the school safety patrol was important. The neighborhood was in the shadow of the world famous Ford Rouge Plant.

Two blocks south of the school ran two very busy thoroughfares, Dix Avenue and Vernor Highway. These two streets were part of a busy commercial center. The streets connected the Rouge Plant and the Salina neighborhood to the great city of Detroit. Trucks of hot slag coming from the factory would go by bellowing hot steam from the slag. Busses, cars, trucks, taxis, and street cars came by in huge numbers. Safeties and an adult supervisor had a huge responsibility in crossing students each day. Through rain and snow the safeties were at their posts. The four boys made sure of that.

Mr. Beckman was the teacher sponsor of the patrol. He preached safety at all times. He was proud of the continuing "no child hurt" during his years of service. He also took good care of the safeties, too. On cold mornings, after arriving from duty, he made sure there was hot chocolate for everyone in the cafeteria before they went to class. On Fridays, he added donuts. There were picnics, a trip to the Ford Rotunda during the Christmas holiday, and one afternoon Detroit Tiger game at Briggs Stadium in the spring. The Rotunda was built for the Chicago World's Fair in 1932. Henry Ford brought it back to Dearborn to be used for expositions. It was quite a place. It was a giant

The Ford Rouge Plant was known as the largest factory in the world.

Ford workers boarding and unloading from street car at Gate 4.

The Ford Rotunda thrilled the children from all over the world.

circle shaped building with the roof done in layers and lit up with bright colors.

At Christmas time, the Rotunda became a Christmas fantasy land. People came from all over the nation to visit the Rotunda. It was an honor to serve on the safety patrol. Each week a safety was chosen as safety boy of the week. At the end of the year, Mr. Beckman would determine who would be safety boy of the year. That, too, was a great honor for a job well done.

The school was the center of life for all the kids. It had quite a history. In 1915, Henry Ford, the famous auto industrialist, purchased a giant piece of land where he would build his Rouge Plant. A school was on that land and served the children of the area and was called the Rouge School. The Rouge School was named for the Rouge River that ran right through the area. The Rouge River was so named by the French because it had a red tone up down the banks as red berries from the many bushes reflected in the water and the fallen berries made the banks reddish in color. So, the French called it Le Rouge or red, in the French language. Mr. Ford had a new school, Salina, built in the neighborhood just east of where the factory was being constructed. It opened in January of 1918. It was a modern two floor and two classroom building and had an office for the principal and custodial area. The Rouge School remained for many years as a small office building for the company after 1918.

During the 1920's, the Rouge Plant began to expand and many people transferred from his Highland Park, Michigan plant — the Rouge was considered the biggest factory in the world. As the company grew, so did the population of the South End. The gang's Salina neighborhood was often referred to as the South End because it was located in the southeast part of Dearborn. Immigrants from all over the world came to the Salina neighborhood. During the 1930's there were more than 40 different nationalities and ethnicities. The most remarkable thing occurred during the many decades that passed. The people liked living in the neighborhood and they liked each other. The kids learned many words of many different languages. They especially leaned the swear words! Oh my! The largest groups over the years were Rumanian, Syrian, Italian, Serbian, Armenian, German, Yugoslavian, Polish, Irish, and Southern American.

Salina Street was the main street for the neighborhood and there were many businesses. Among them were: Tripepi's, Chungo's Market, Al's Little Confectionary, the Salina Restaurant, Ted's Market, the Fordson Bazzar, and other mom and pop operations. On holidays, each of the business owners would put an American flag on a pole at the front of the sidewalk, near the curb, outside of their establishment. Looking down Salina Street from the school was a glorious and patriotic sight to see as the flags were blowing in the wind. There was a neighborhood swimming pool, a Boys Club, a giant hill to sled, and an area of natural pond where kids would ice skate in winter and catch frogs and tad poles in summer. In this neighborhood of many nationalities the kids all had one thing in common — they loved America. Their parents made sure that the kids understood how great it was to be an American.

During the Christmas holiday, the city would string colorful lights from telephone pole to telephone pole. The mayor had the city workers wrap Christmas evergreen garland around each pole. So beautiful! The city had a great mayor who loved kids and Christmas. Standing on the corner from Vernor and looking north down Salina at night when the lights were on, one would see a dazzling display of multicolored lights zigzagging from one side of the street to the other — pole to pole. Hanging on the stringed lights were large illuminated Christmas candy canes, toys, and Santas. So delightful!

The two-room Salina School built in, 1918, became too small for the community and was replaced by a much bigger building. Mr. Hotchkiss and Miss Henn, the first principal and first teacher, watched as the new school was built and made ready for a growing community. Miss Henn was the original teacher from the Rouge School and Mr. Hotchkiss came to open the bigger Salina School. This began a new era where lifelong friendships and school love would prevail. Never was the saying, "Be true to your school," more important to students than at Salina.

Mr. Hotchkiss had the demeanor and look of a stern principal. He was six feet four inches tall, lanky with a narrow face that appeared stern at all times. He wore glasses and had brown hair and later — very white hair. His leadership over the years created an academic and educational environment that was outstanding. Miss Henn was very attractive, strong willed, intelligent, and kind. Together, they set the example for all of the students from the 1920's through the 1950's. Many students became successful in virtually all the professions.

Salina School was a beautiful building with the center built first and wings added in 1926 to accommodate the growing student population. The center of the building was three floors with many classrooms, a gym with three balconies and stage, large cafeteria, auditorium, home economics rooms, offices, and custodial quarters. By 1926, new wings added thirty new classrooms, a new main office, nurse's quarters, library, kindergarten rooms, and science rooms. There was a counseling area,

supply room, text book storage room, large teachers' lounge, projection room behind the rear balcony, and several general offices. In 1951, a band and vocal music wing was added.

The two glorious kindergarten rooms were enormous and every student who experienced these rooms reminisce how beautiful they were. During the Great Depression, famed illustrator, Edward McCandlish was commissioned to paint murals of children's nursery

rhyme characters and depictions. A child only need to look up to see life sized Humpty Dumpty, Little Boy Blue, The Old Lady in the Shoe, Little Jack Horner, Mary Had a Little Lamb, and Little Bo Peep, and so many more come to life. The murals adorned the walls of the whole kindergarten. The kindergarten was a child's fantasy wonderland where a child could immerse herself in the world of children's song and literature.

The murals amazed and bewildered generations of children. They continue to adorn the kindergarten rooms today.

Grass grew healthy and green with bushes and trees dotting the entire front of the building. A flag pole, taller than the three story building, was in the center facing the building. The bars the gang would sit on every day encircled each section of the lawn. It was against the rules to walk on the grass. Mr. Hotchkiss was a stickler for that. The bars extended from the building to the sidewalk and then lined the sidewalk facing the street. The bars were three inches in circumference, eighteen inches off the ground, made of hard hollow steel, and made perfect places to sit and hang out.

The school faced Salina Street and was named for the salt mines that lay beneath the whole neighborhood which extended many miles under the whole area. The back of the school faced Wyoming Avenue and the eight giant Ford smoke stacks atop the power plant would be bellowing smoke night and day. There was plenty of playground space, too. After school and on weekends and summer, lots of baseball and other activities were played on the large playground. The gang would choose up teams and the first chant you would hear is, "No chips on broken windows." If they broke a window, everyone ran like the dickens. During the school day, one never crossed in the grassy areas. The only person ever seen on the grass was the safety who would put up the flag each and every day. One could see the flag blowing in the wind from a very far distance.

Mr. Hotchkiss was an environmentalist and loved flowers. He would come around to every classroom each spring to supply students with flower and vegetable seeds to be planted and grown each year. He was very well respected and loved but absolutely stern. He administered with tough love. He also had a black leather strap that he used as often as was necessary. If a student walked on the grass and it was reported by the safety, it was considered a demerit. Demerits were basic infractions of the rules. J-walking, running in the hallways, excessive horseplay, being tardy to class — and other inappropriate behaviors were considered demerits. Three demerits meant the safety would go to the student's class and escort the student to the office and Mr. Hotchkiss or

Mr. Dobronski, assistant principal, would administer punishment. The student might have to pick up trash around the school using a broom stick with a nail on the end to stick the paper and put it in a barrel. Mr. Hotchkiss might even take out the "strap." Ouch! The safety boys that brought kids to Mr. Hotchkiss for walking on the grass — would play football, run races, and all sorts of other games on the grass when school was out. The gang lived close to school, so more than anyone else, was guilty of playing on the grass — after school. Go figure.

The front of the school was a place to hang out when there was no school. The gang played a game called hurdles with the bars. Starting at the side street, they would race jumping and hurdling all seven bars to determine the winner. Phillip, the "Bugman" usually won. That is, when his older brother Edward wasn't there. Edward was as fast as lightening in a storm. They called Phil that because he played tenacious defense in basketball. Someone said he guarded his man and was all over him like a bug. So he became known as the "Bugman." A boy named Morris could walk the bars just like a circus tightrope walker. He could walk forward and backward and keep it up all day. Some of the kids could walk and hold their balance a little, but nothing like Morris. After a hard day, the gang would buy a Pepsi and a bag of chips and sit at the middle stairs planning the next activity.

The center of the front of the school was referred to as the middle stairs. There were seven steps leading up to the doors and into the building. Those seven steps served the gang well. The boys played a game called "Three Flies Up." It was a variation of baseball. It could be played one against one, or two against two. The batting team (there was no bat) was a player who would face the stairs and throw the ball aiming for the first, second, or third stair. Catching the very corner or tip of the step allowed the ball to have velocity and rise up into the air. If the ball made it to the street, it was a "grandslam." There was danger since local traffic went up and down Salina Street throughout the day. This included the Intertown Bus Company and delivery trucks of all sorts. The gang made a rule; if the ball was heading for a homerun into

The middle stairs bounded by the bars. Hundreds of pictures were taken of students at the stairs throughout Salina's history. Kids could walk these bars like a circus performer on a tightrope.

the street, the defensive player could not step in the street to catch it. This was a safety precaution so that he would not blindly back into the street and step into oncoming traffic. A grounder, line-drive, or pop-up, fielded properly was an out. If it got by the fielder, or if he made an error, it was a run. There were no singles, doubles, or triples. Either a homerun or a grand slam counted as a score. If the ball hit the step and inverted back toward the building it was an out. If it inverted and hit the building, and the fielder caught it coming off the wall it was a double play. What a game it was. It honed the baseball skills of the players. The gang learned to field to their left and back hand to the right. It was very competitive and lots of fun. A rubber ball was used for the game but sometimes-a tennis ball was substituted. The tennis ball really livened up the game.

The gang was in junior high. It was getting close to the end of the school year. There were several end-of–the-year festivities yet to be completed. Among the activities were the clean-up parade, safety patrol picnic at Camp Dearborn, the ninth grade graduation, and the

Sunset Dance.

The gang had been secretly planning to raft the River Rouge when school was out. They had drawn up plans and began building a raft that none of their parents, teachers, or anyone else were aware. Their goal was to reach Greenfield Village (where America's history has been preserved), stopping at Fordson Island, and passing Fairlane Mansion where Henry Ford lived. It was to be an adventure to remember. The summer of 1955 would change them forever.

While they were building the raft, Dr. Bones (Robert), the dreamer and inventor, told them he was building a Time Machine. He explained that when he finished, it would be able to take them back in time and back again to 1955. He kept telling everyone that by turning this dial and that dial and setting a date and pushing a button — poof off they would go. The gang didn't take him serious but no one took him serious when he created a hot air balloon that carried him as high as the top of the school and landed him in a very tall oak tree. His picture ended up on the front page of the Detroit Times. What a sight to see as he was dangling for dear life and his Pop was down on the ground looking as the fireman brought him down. His behind was kind of sore after this escapade. Tough love!

The mayor of the city was big on keeping the city clean. The South End was the industrial portion of the city where several smaller plants were located. He really concentrated on this industrial neighborhood. He coined the phrase, "Help Keep Dearborn Clean." It was printed on trash cans, signs, buildings, police cars and on park benches. The mayor created a job for a man who was out of work. He had a push wagon with a big barrel and brooms, shovels, and dustpans. He would push it through the neighborhood everyday sweeping and cleaning. The man was so grateful he named his son after the mayor.

On the morning of the parade the gang met at the store. The parade was a big deal. All the students from all the classrooms would participate — more than a thousand kids! It was a kindergarten through ninth grade effort. As they were looking out of the store window, right at the school, Neemer asked Charles if he remembered when they took a little kid, who was up in the tree next to the school, safely down. This was by the north entrance next to Tripepi's.

"Yeah, I do," he replied. "We had a heck of a time getting him out of that tree. He climbed right to the top. Remember what he said when we asked him his name?" continued Charles.

"Yep! He kept saying, 'Me monkey, me monkey!' over and over again," said Neemer.

"I remember what you told him. You said, 'Ok monkey, come on down' and finally he did. From that time on, he was known as Monkey!" Everyone laughed but it was true.

Sophie, the owner of the store was looking forward to parade day. It meant she would have a huge business day. The mayor always bought ice cream for the kids after the parade. People would come and go from the store all day. She sold hot dogs for 10 cents. It was half a hot dog with mustard and onion and wrapped in deli paper. Delicious! She sold, "Oh So" soda pop for a nickel. The cream filled bun was 6 cents. What a deal and what great eating! Her helpers were her daughters Suzie, Rosa, and son Rocco. When you walked in, to the left and in the corner was the booth. Kids carved their names in the table top. In front of the booth was the candy showcase. For a penny you could buy a Black Jack, or a squirrel, or a slice of coconut watermelon. There were so many candies like Chum Gum, red hot jaw breakers, baseball cards with bubble gum, Mary Janes, and much, much more. Big candy bars were a nickel.

The unique thing about the store was the kids could go there for lunch during the school day. There was a bubble gum machine that sat against the wall right as one walks in the door. For a penny, the kids would watch a red toy dump truck make a circular motion and stop half-way at the "bubble gum drop hopper" and the hopper would release a marble size bubble gum. The truck would continue along to complete the circle and stop and dump the prized gum. Sophie was really smart. She loved to make money. The more bubble gum the kids bought the more the machine made a profit. She had the hopper filled with several speckled bubble gums. If the kid buying the gum got a speckled gum, she redeemed it for five cents worth of candy from the showcase. A couple of the boys were smart, too. So they thought! They discovered by looking really close through the glass they could tell when the speckled gum was next in the hopper. All of a sudden the same boys were winning the bonus candy. Sophie finally caught on and there was a price to pay!

Several other games amused the gang that hung out at Tripepi's. There was the baseball pinball machine. It was extremely popular and it sat right near the booth. There was a counter penny arcade type machine. It was 18 inches wide and 24 inches tall with a glass front. Inside the glass were dozens and dozens of one inch type steel prongs. The prongs were secured through the back of the machine in rows that zig-zagged. By turning the knob on the right, and releasing a small steel ball, a four inch football player was able to kick it with force. It would go straight up and over tumbling

The kick and catch counter game provided fun for the kids. Just a penny!

downward. Looking through the glass and watching it fall, it zigged and zagged and would go left and then right and then left and so on. The player would turn the knob on the left moving a player trying to catch the ball. Catching the ball earned a point and a free kick, Once three balls were dropped the game was over. This was a very skillful game. Competition between the kids in this neighborhood was a way of life. It did not matter what game was being played; winning was absolutely important.

That morning, before the parade, while the safety captain and lieutenant made their rounds checking on safeties and cruising the playground and school ground, many activities were taking place. Everyone walked to school and got there early to hang out or play. Some kids were pitching pennies against the wall of the school. The person pitching the penny would stand eight or ten feet away from the wall and pitch it trying to get as close to the wall as possible when the penny came to rest. The next player would toss and then the next and so on. The person whose penny was closest to the wall won all the pennies that were pitched. A leaner (if the penny somehow was pitched and ended leaning against the wall) was the winner and paid double.

Since it was the day of the parade the safeties had to be vigilant. They had to get "tough' with the penny pitchers who didn't want to quit. It was the same guys all the time who would pitch pennies. The game was a form of gambling. Sometimes the game escalated to nickels and lots of lunch money would be lost. Reporting them would have meant visiting Mr. Hotchkiss and getting the razor strap or being suspended or both. Dino was the leader and refused to quit.

"You can't tell us what to do," he said.

"Dino is right, it's none of your business what we do," said his buddy, Mike Hisely.

"Yes it is," replied Alan. "When we're on duty, it is our business. After school or on the weekends you can do whatever you want."

Hisely was a real trouble maker. He could never be trusted. He wanted to fight. These guys were the school tough guys or "bullies." Alan didn't want to fight but he stood up to him and held his ground. He and Alan went nose to nose. Sometimes muscle was the only way to handle a problem. Mike would back down every time. That was good because Alan was in the right. Besides, Alan could take him easy. The safeties were not only the best athletes in the school but the toughest, too. They always stuck together no matter what the situation. If they had to fight — they did.

Neemer and Phil were walking by the middle stairs and saw the sixth and seventh graders playing a game of "frozen tag." The players had to stay within the boundaries of the middle stairs. Seven or ten people played with two being "it." When they tagged a player he was frozen. When all the players were frozen, the first two tagged were now it. But the fun came when a player was frozen and an unfrozen player who could reach them would free them by touching them. Strategy in catching everyone was necessary.

"Relea-So" was being played on the playground. Ten or more players played and two were "it" like in frozen tag. But with Relea-So, the tagged player was brought to "jail" where the other tagged players were. It was a confined area by the building with a circle drawn in the gravel creating the jail. If a free player was able to get to jail fast enough to beat the chaser and not be tagged, he would yell "Relea-So," and everyone scattered. Great fun!

Since it was almost the beginning of summer the rhubarb plants were ready to harvest. Mrs. Hill had a big crop of fresh grown rhubarb from her green house. She sold them for a penny a piece. The leaf was very big and green and the rhubarb stalk resembled celery. But it had a completely different taste. It was sour. Really sour! The kids would buy salted pumpkin seeds and eat them along with the rhubarb. Sour and good — so they said. The rhubarb business was really brisk on this parade day as a lot of kids were coming from Mrs. Hill's big garden and greenhouse.

The nine o'clock bell rang and the students reported to class to make ready for the parade. The assistant principal, Mr. Dobronski, read the morning bulletin over the school intercom system.

"Good morning students and staff and welcome. Today is one of the special days of our school year at Salina. Mr. Hotchkiss has reminded me to tell all students to be on your best behavior as you prepare for the parade. All the floats are made and ready to be placed in line. Our visiting dignitaries include the mayor, members of the board of education, members of the city council, and the police chief.

The Dearborn Guide Newspaper photographer will be here, too. The Salina, Clean-up Paint-up Fix-up parade is the biggest and best in the whole city. Please listen to your teacher's directions as you make ready today. A very special surprise is in order for all of us today. It is a secret and no one knows but Mr. Hotchkiss, Mr. Legrew, and me. I promise you will be thrilled. So, don't ask me what it is; we promise all of you will be surprised and happy. I have asked Robert Simon, from the Junior Red Cross Club, to lead us in the Pledge of Allegiance."

He thanked Robert after the Pledge and said the parade was scheduled to begin at 1:30 in the afternoon. He reminded all staff and students of their responsibilities in order to have a successful parade. He finished by saying, "Let's have a great Salina day and make this parade the best ever." He added: "I would like to meet with the student government leadership in my office at 10 am."

The safeties put up the flag each morning and took it down at the end of school. They had to go into a classroom on the second floor and open a window and unclasp the flagpole line. Usually the rope from a flag pole would be wrapped on the pole. But at Salina, during off school hours, kids would take the rope and swing round and round on it. Nadeen and Chris had the responsibility that week of doing the flag. Mr. Beckman rotated the raising and lowering of flag among all the safeties. Everyone was trained on the proper folding of the flag and reminded never to let it touch the ground. On this particular day, Chris and Nay (his nickname) added the Michigan State Flag as well as the Salina Wildcat Pennant Flag. Together, way up in the sky, the three flags watched over the school and parade as they flew in the breeze.

The city vehicles had started to arrive and some of the safeties were out welcoming them. The drivers of the different vehicles and other visitors were escorted to the cafeteria where the home economics club served rolls, donuts, and coffee. They brought two fire trucks, a police car, a gigantic street sweeper, and a truck that spread water from spigots on the side of the truck. There would be some convertible automobiles to carry the parade queen and her court and different floats created by the clubs. The mayor had arrived and his official city car was placed in line, too. The mayor would walk the parade and wave to all the citizens along the parade route. He was a great mayor and everyone liked him. Miss Henn and Mr. Hotchkiss rode in the Mayor's car.

Meanwhile, Mr. Dobronski was meeting with the student council members. It consisted of the school mayor, a judge, a treasurer, and secretary. Only ninth graders could run for office. All the junior high students had a voice and vote for who would be the school governmental leaders. They discussed the parade and the rest of the end of school activities. Lee, the mayor, delegated to each of the council members responsibilities to oversee each of the remaining activities. After it adjourned, Mr. Hotchkiss and Mr. Dobronski had a closed door session with the mayor. They invited Lee, the school mayor, and Miss Johnson, school secretary to attend. The principals believed in developing leadership at Salina, knowing the future belonged to them.

With a 1:30 start time, the school was all abuzz with activities everywhere on the campus. Lunch was moved up in order to get the parade started on time. The students began making their way out to the assembling area. They lined up according to grade level. First came the dignitaries and the vehicles, the marching band was next, and the convertibles used for the court behind the band. The kindergartners had signs saying, "Keep Our Neighborhood Clean." First and second graders rode tricycles and pulled wagons. Third, fourth, and fifth graders were allowed to ride their bikes. They were all decorated with balloons and streamers. Many of the kids tied balloons to the back of the frame where the axle of wheel is and flipped them under and over allowing the balloons to rub against the spokes as the wheel turned. This made the bicycles sound like motorcycles. Varoom!

Just before the parade began, Mr. Hotchkiss announced the results of the voting for 1955 clean-up queen. When he announced Lila's name, the students cheered with thunderous clapping and shouted lots of hoorays. She was very beautiful and extremely nice to everyone. She would be a fabulous highlight in this year's parade.

Still, the secret surprise that Mr. Dobronski had talked about was just that — a secret! All the students were in suspense and talking and wondering what was going to happen. Was there going to be a famous celebrity? They knew the parade ended with ice cream and treats so that wasn't it.

Mr. Dobronski was affectionately called CRD (his initials) by his colleagues and his students. He was a great man — smart, a gifted former pro athlete, and terrific with the student body. No one messed around when it came to CRD. Everyone knew better. He was fair but he was tough. When he played pick-up basketball, football, or baseball, with the gang — he was in it to win. He and Coach Costea were instrumental in teaching them how to play. They inherited from both of them and Mr. Berce, the math teacher, the will to win.

"CRD," Neemer called out. "Can Alan and I see you a minute? Would you step into our office?"

"What office?" he demanded to know. "Now you guys have an office?"

"Just kidding, CRD, just kidding," they replied.

"Tell us, what's up today with the secret? We promise not tell anyone."

"Oh, you promise not to tell?"

"We gotta' know," they said.

"Oh, you gotta' know, eh? Here's what you "gotta" know. Get back to business and get ready for the parade. How's that for knowing," he said emphatically.

The boys actually did have an office and a key to go with it for their weekly safety meetings. It was between the second and third floors on the landing which was used to store AVI equipment. They skedaddled back to class. Mrs. Renko, their homeroom teacher, was giving directions. She directed those students marching with the band should report to the band room. Students who were part of different organizations like the cheerleaders, safeties, hall monitors, AVI Club, and Junior Red Cross would go to their respective areas.

The home economics club was busy making pop corn and red candy apples. The combination of these treats being made created a delightful aroma throughout the whole school. These treats were a regular every Thursday treat that students could buy as they went home at the end of the school day. The girls in the club were ready to sell to their classmates and all of the spectators along the parade route.

The sounds of music, horns, sirens, bells, and shouts of happiness could be heard as the students and parade participants lined up to start the parade. Several of the football team and cheerleaders dressed like clowns and intended to hand out packets of flower seeds and suckers along the parade route. Mr. Hotchkiss was big on flowers!

The parade began on time heading down Lowrey Street and then turning on to Holly Street. It proceeded down to Lapeer, then to Roulo, and west on Eagle. Heading down Eagle the parade would turn on to Salina Street on its way back to the school. Each group of marchers had banners attached to poles colorfully painted with slogans of keeping the neighborhood clean and tidy. Mr. Faes and the band were always impressive. The Salina band always scored high in state junior high band competitions with Mr. Faes as band director. The mayor and

The Salina School Marching Band leads the parade.

Students with Clean Up-Paint-Up-Fix Up signs.

City water truck joins the parade.

his department heads were busy waving to the crowds along the way. Politicians love parades. The mayor's face beamed and beamed. He especially loved the parade. Why not, all the parents and citizens were voters who kept him in office. "Hooray, Mr. Mayor!"

The parade turned on to Salina Street back toward the school and

The band heads down Holly Street.

The Safety Patrol lines up to take their place in the parade.

the middle stairs where the podium and microphone were set up for the mayor and Mr. Hotchkiss to address the crowd. As the band led the parade down Salina, they passed many of the business along the way. All the workers from Al's Market came out and waved. The patrons

The litter bugs being escorted by the police as students don costumes for the parade.

Members of the queen and her court wearing lovely dresses and waving to the crowd.

of the Bogolia's department store, the taverns, the coffee houses, post office, and hotels, all came out to watch and wave to the marchers. The flags were put out by all the businesses and homes along Salina. It was quite a sight to see. American style! As the parade passed Omar

Homeroom 312 is well represented in the parade.

Boy Scout Troop D 33 marches proudly proclaiming keeping your neighborhood clean has no language. Students of many heritages are part of the parade.

Street, there were the Russian Club, Ted's Meat Market, and the Salina Restaurant where many Turkish, Armenian, and Syrian World War One veterans would come to eat and play cards.

The gang really enjoyed walking into the Salina restaurant during hot summer days. It was jam-packed with old men. The owner was, Mr. Mustache, at least that's what the gang called him, because he had a long bushy gray mustache. He would give each of them a cold glass of water and big smile. They waited at the counter where the water spigot was and where the men sat on stools to be served. There was a back room where men could be seen playing cards. Lamb shank stew with generous portions of lamb and rice was the main meal each day. The men ate their food with Syrian bread. It was 10 inches in diameter and you could cut it in half and it would open like a pocket. When the gang was hungry, they ordered French fries and the cook put them inside the "pocket." They smothered it with ketsup. Once, the gang asked Mr. Mustache where this bread came from. He said it was bread that was brought to America by immigrants from Syria. That is why it was called Syrian bread. The gang never forgot what he said:

"Boys, it was the kind of bread that Jesus ate at the Last Supper."

The Fordson Bazaar was on the left just passed the restaurant. Jimmy and his mother operated the store. They were Jewish and always greeted kids with a smile. They had an apartment in the back of the store. Jimmy worked at Ford Motor Company and his mother operated the store during the day. It was a marvelous small department store where one could by most anything. Kids bought their Christmas presents each year to share with classmates.

When the band reached Chungo's Market, the most unbelievable thing happened. Looking down Salina from the front of the parade was a glorious sight. One could see everything. The American flags were in front of all of the businesses all the way down Salina to Eagle. The breeze was just right and the flags were waving in the air. Boy Scout Troop D33 was led by their flag carriers. Bright colorful balloons could be seen everywhere. The band was playing the song, "My Country Tis of Thee" when all of a sudden, the sky and the whole street seemed to rock with thunder. The street was vibrating. There was a booming roar of engines and everyone thought it was one of those new guided

The secret was out. Mr. Legrew flew his Sabre Jet right down Salina Street.

missiles. It was an F 86 Sabre Jet Fighter roaring right down Salina Street just above the heads of all of those marching and all of those watching the parade.

The noise reverberated throughout the whole neighborhood. The marchers, the parents, the teachers, and the mayor couldn't believe it. They were all awe-struck. This narrow neighborhood street suddenly came alive as this fighter jet zoomed over head. There he was, the great teacher, Major Richard Legrew, of the United States Air Force, piloting that fighter jet just above the marchers. He waved and swayed his wings up and down as if to say "hello" fighter jet style. So cool! Everyone could see him smiling. Everyone felt as though they could reach up and grab the jet. As he flew down Salina, he veered to the left climbing high on his way back to Selfridge Air Base. What a moment in time that was for the community! Mr. Legrew was a fighter pilot during the Korean War from 1951 to 1953. The students were laughing, cheering, whistling, and clapping, as they watched the trail of smoke the jet left behind.

The parade ended at the middle stairs as the band assembled in front of the school and the invited guests took their place up near the podium. The mayor went straight to the podium near the microphone while the students, parents, and everyone gathered around to watch and listen.

"Mr. Hotchkiss and Mr. Dobronski, it is has been the most thrilling parade of my entire public life. When you told me this morning there would be a special surprise during the parade, I had no idea such a spine-tingling and exciting event was to take place. You must give my best wishes and thanks to Mr. Legrew when he returns from the air base. He has helped to make this parade the best ever. Wasn't it great kids?' The students went ballistic with applause and whistles. "Boys and girls and ladies and gentleman, you are so lucky to be part of such a great community and school. I always love to come to Salina and visit with all of my friends here. There are so many different nationalities in this neighborhood and I enjoy eating all the different foods, as you can see (the mayor was a bit pudgy). Thank you for the wonderful luncheon, too. Miss Iris, you have done a wonderful job coordinating the parade, thank you. Boys and girls you must help your parents keep the lawns nice and trimmed. If you can plant a vegetable and flower garden around your yard, it will help make the neighborhood even brighter. Always remember to put trash where it belongs…in a trash barrel. Mr. Hotchkiss, I would like to say thank you once again for inviting me today."

Mr. Hotchkiss came to the podium and shook hands with the mayor. "Thank you, mayor, for joining us today at the annual Salina Clean-up, Paint-up, Fix-up Parade. Let's hear it boys and girls through your applause how much we appreciate the mayor visiting with us."

A rousing round of applause and cheering could be heard all around the outside of the school. The mayor waved thanks to the crowd.

"Boys and girls how about that jet plane flown by Mr. Legrew? Wasn't it inspiring?" asked Mr. Hotchkiss. Again, the students and guests cheered. "Mr. Legrew wanted me to share some of his experiences while in the service during the Korean War. He flew several missions during the war. He was also acquainted with some of the great pilots during the war. He knew a great deal about James Jabara, an ace during the war. Peter Fernandez, Gabby Gabrecki, Joe McConnel, John Glenn, and Buzz Aldrin were also distinguished flyers. Pilots Glen and Aldrin would say that someday they might very well fly into outer space on a rocket ship. So, even though Mr. Legrew isn't here, let us show our appreciation by giving him a tremendous ovation."

Just then the mayor whispered something to Mr. Hotchkiss. Mr. Hotchkiss nodded his head as if to say, "Yes, sir, Mr. Mayor."

"Boys and girls, as soon as you put all of the equipment away, I declare with the mayor's approval that you have the rest of the school day off." The kids went wild. "And, oh yes, the mayor has invited all of you to enjoy all the ice cream you can eat. It will be his treat."

What an afternoon and what a way to end the school day. All the kids enjoyed being part of the parade and especially loved the ice cream. Why naturally!

The gang met at Tripepi's store that evening. Everyone seemed to be busy playing the games and listening to music. There was a new game brought in. It stood about five and a half feet tall and had an air rifle attached to a handle facing the glass in front of it. There were a dozen balls made of sponge that sat in round half pockets looking straight at the front of the glass. There were many more pockets than balls. When a coin was inserted, the player got five shots. Each shot aimed at any of the balls would release all the balls flying sporadically. It was like molecules diffusing. To get a clearer picture of how this game went, picture putting 20 mouse traps on a board and stapling each trap to the board. Then set each trap and put a ping pong ball where the cheese would go. Suddenly you release one trap and all the balls go flying every which way as each trap springs into action. A player earned points and extra shots if the balls landed diagonally or corner to corner. If they landed in a straight line, across or up or down, they were awarded points and a free shot. If each corner and the very middle pocket contained a ball, the player won a free game.

Alan was in a giddy mood and leaned over reminding Neemer about the parade and how beautiful the parade queen, Lila, looked.

"She sure was beautiful," said Neemer. "At the Sunset dance, I am going to ask her to dance with me. A slow dance — know what I mean?"

"Don't get fresh with her or her brother Sam will know — exactly what you mean!" replied Alan.

"I promise to be a good boy," Neemer said. "Why naturally," they both chimed.

Pat and Lynn walked in and said hello to all of the guys. Charles could see they were a bit upset and a little shaken.

"What's wrong?" asked Charles.

"Nothing," replied Pat.

"Yes, there is something wrong. Hey guys, come here," he told them.

"What's up?" they asked.

"That's what I am trying to find out. Come on girls, spill it. What has happened?" Charles asked again.

"Well, we were walking down Lapeer passed the pool and Dino and his buddies came up on us and started bothering us," said Lynn.

"We told them to get lost and stop pestering us," Pat said.

"They started getting bolder and bolder and tried to put their arms around us trying to kiss us," said the girls.

"I slapped Dino and Lynn kicked Hisley and we started running," said Pat.

"Where are they?" asked Phil.

"We saw them go into Crazy Helen's store," they replied.

"Let's go gang," said Phil.

"Yeah, let's go take care of this," they all agreed.

"Forget it guys. We don't want more trouble," said Pat.

"That's not the point," said Charles. "If they get away with it now they're going to do it again," he added.

The gang walked down to Crazy Helen's and looked in the window and saw them sitting and drinking a Pepsi. One of them was at the juke box looking at the song titles.

"Dino, Mike, and your other buddy, come on out we want to see you," yelled one of the fellows.

They came out and in a sarcastic manner, Dino says, "What the heck do you want?"

"What we want," said Neemer, as he jumps right into Dino's face, "is for all of you to stop bothering Lynn and Pat."

"That's none of your business, or yours, or yours," said Dino as he pointed at them.

"We mean it. They're nice girls and our friends and we aren't going to let punks like you harass them or bother them. Remember, we aren't in school now," said Charles.

Mike looked at Alan and said, "Do you think I forgot what you said today before school?"

Just as soon as he said it, he shoved Alan. That was the wrong thing to do. Boom! A right cross to the jaw and down goes Mike. Phil sees Dino reach for Alan and fires off another punch. Boom! The punch lands under Dino's chin and he goes down. Just then the other kid started running and didn't look back. When the two boys got up, they weren't so brave anymore.

"The next time you see those girls, you both better apologize. Because if you don't," and repeating again, "if you don't, we will be back to settle the score once and for all. Is that clear? Am I right guys?" asked Alan.

"Yessiree Bob," said the boys. "We will make them sorry they ever moved to this neighborhood," they said.

"One more thing, mister big shot, Dino. In school, we are tired of all the headaches you and your guys cause everyone. So, do not get out of line here or in school. If you do," he repeats again, "if you do, we will come back and clean your clock," said Charles.

"I'll tell Mr. Dobronski that you are threatening us," screamed Dino.

"Go ahead and tell him. He'll just tell us to give it you — but good," answered Neemer.

When they got back to Tripepi's, Neemer shouted, "I'm buying pop for everyone."

Alan walked over to him, tilted his head, looked him straight in the eyes and said, "Did I hear you right? Hey everyone, did I get that clear what he said? He's buying?" He looked again at Neemer and said jubilantly, "My man!" Good friends!

"O.K. guys, come over here and sit down," said Charles. They walked over and sat at the booth. Pat and Lynn joined in, too.

"We still have lots of work to do on the raft so we better set a plan for tomorrow," he continued.

"What raft?" asked Lynn. No one said anything since they hadn't told anyone yet. Lynn asked again, "What raft?" Again silence.

"Alright guys, what are you talking about — a raft? Where is it? What are going to do with it? We want to help," said Pat.

"Not only do we want to help, we want to go with you guys wherever you are going," Lynn said firmly.

"It's really a secret," said Alan.

"You can't keep a secret from us. We're part of the gang. We're cool, man! You dig? We are going," demanded Pat.

"Look guys, you just stood up for us. We are just like family. You protected us from those bad guys and now you won't tell us? You got to," said Lynn. They were part of the gang. Pat was pretty. She was tall with black hair and deep blue eyes. She was a great athlete and excellent swimmer. Lynn was just as pretty, smart, and had blond hair and sky blue eyes.

The guys looked at each other for a moment and each shrugged their shoulders as if to say, "OK, you can go."

"We'll tell you. But, you're both sworn to secrecy," said Charles. "Agreed?"

"Cross our hearts and hope to die," they both said.

"We're going to sail the River Rouge," stated Alan.

"Wow, how neat. Thanks guys. We'll do our part," the girls said. The gang left for home.

The whole school was anxiously awaiting the end of the year festivities as the last day of school was drawing near. Still left, were the ninth grade graduation, the Sunset Dance, and the trip to Camp Dearborn for the safeties and hall monitors.

On Monday morning, the gang met early at Gene's, the confectionary across from the school. Gene and Beaula opened early in the morning where dads and moms going to work could stop in for fresh coffee and baked donuts. Beaula, Gene's wife, was extremely nice and a quite reserved lady. She was an expert baker and the baked goods were a great hit — especially in the morning. After school she charged only half price to kids so that she could sell them all.

The store had three steps to walk up before entering. There was a large counter straight ahead. The counter had stools where kids could sit and enjoy a fountain coke or drink a Sweet Sixteen bottle of pop. Sweet Sixteen was a sixteen ounce bottle of soda pop that could be purchased in many flavors. Behind the counter were the coolers for milk, pop, and other refrigerated goods. Also, behind the counter, was a door that led to the apartment in back of the store where Gene and Beaula lived. To the right, walking in, was a double showcase where candy bars and all sorts of other penny candies could be seen for purchase. The second showcase held the baked goods like donuts, cookies, and breads. The potato chip rack was on the wall behind the candy showcase. To the left was the juke box. In this neighborhood, every store of this type had a juke box and the kids would dance to the latest Rock 'n' Roll hits. Two of the most popular dances were the "Chicken" and the "Half-Time." The chicken was a fast paced dance where the kids would heel toe right foot and heel toe left while both elbows would sway like chicken wings. Their hands would be in a loose fist. It was a great dance. It was popular across the country. The half-time was a variation of the "Jitter-Bug." It was the favorite dance for the kids except for a slow dance. But of course! Gene made sure the kids were well behaved and did not get carried away. School did not start until nine and the older kids gathered at Gene's.

"So we have graduation on Wednesday, Camp Dearborn on Thursday, and the Sunset Dance on Friday night," said Pat.

"Yeah," said Alan. "I wonder who is going to win the Martin Award."

"Don't forget the Roosevelt Award, Alan," said Phil.

"Yeah, the Roosevelt Award will go to the highest grade point achievers and the Martin will go the student who has achieved success against difficult odds and who showed leadership and outstanding effort through junior high," he added.

"I can't wait for Camp Dearborn," said Charles

"Me, too," added Lynn. "We get to eat all the ice cream, chips, and pop we want!"

"The Sunset Dance will be the coolest of all time," said Neemer.

"Why?" asked Pat.

"Cuz', we'll be there, silly."

"Oh, yeah, you're right," she said smiling.

"After all of this, gang, we begin the plan to sail the Rouge," said Charles.

"Right, it'll be really cool," they all harmonized together.

Monday morning of the last week meant the start of packing up classrooms, checking the books in, covering shelves for the summer, and making ready for the events to come. Mrs. Renko and Mr. Randall were the lead teachers of the graduating classes. Mrs. Renko read the morning bulletin to the students before they went to the first hour session. She called off the names of students who were in choir and band to let them know they would practice for the graduation during the fifth and sixth hour class. She reminded all the students to take their text books to each class to be turned in. Mr. DeKay, teacher and counselor, was a stickler for books being in good shape. Each teacher would collect the books one at a time and go through them to make sure they were not damaged, marked in, or had missing pages. By Tuesday morning, the books would then be brought to the book storage room on the second floor and stored there for safe keeping until school started again in the fall. The bell rang and the students left homeroom for the first hour class.

When Charles got to Mr. DeKay's class, Mr. DeKay sent him to get a record book he needed. He knocked on Mr. Dobronski's door.

"Yes, come in. Hi, Charles what do you need?"

"Mr. DeKay needs a record book and he sent me down to get it for him."

"OK. Sit down a minute and I will get one from my file cabinet."

"That's really a nice ash tray on your desk CRD. I made one just like it metal shop. In fact it was a class project for all of us to make one." The ash tray was made of copper with four thimble sized legs brazed on the bottom. It was an ideal ash tray for him because he liked to smoke a pipe. "Mine got lost or misplaced in the metal shop. Mr. Slagle could not find it when I went back to pick it up."

"My little buddy Dino gave this to me. He told me it was a gift for me from him for all the grief during the school year he caused me."

"You don't have to tell me about Dino, CRD. He gives everybody grief. Can I see how he brazed the legs on it and if he shined it on the polishing wheel?"

"Sure, go ahead. I haven't used it yet." While Mr. Dobronski went to the file to get the record book, Charles took a good look at it.

When he returned, Charles said, "Mr. Dobronski, I got some bad news for you."

"Why, what is the matter?" asked CRD.

"Dino didn't make that ash tray. I did. Turn it over and look at the bottom closely and you see my initials and the number 24 on it." He turned it over and sure enough there were the initials and the number 24. "24 is my basketball uniform number," said Charles.

"Oh, my word," said CRD. What will I do with this boy." He sat down and stared out the window looking disappointed. His office window looked into the playground where kids play during recess.

"Mr. Dobronski, don't worry about it. Let's forget it. You know, Dino does cause a lot of trouble but it is not all his fault. His mom and dad are never home and he pretty much is on his own. I don't mind if you don't."

"Thank you young man and well said. Let's keep it our secret." He smiled and shook hands with him and sent him back to class.

The gang stayed in for lunch to enjoy salmon patties and vegetables a favorite at the school. The cafeteria was quite large and was on the third floor of the school. The teachers had a lunch room for themselves just inside the entrance door. Jeff Durbin was part of the AVI club that was responsible for showing movies, handling stage lights, and pretty much anything to do with audio or movies. Lunch was almost an hour long. Kids could go home and get back, stay and eat in the cafeteria by bringing their lunch or buying one. Others went to Sophie's for hot dogs, chips, pop, and a bun. Jeff brought the record player and the kids could listen to the records and dance if they wanted to.

"What song do you want to hear," hollered out Jeff.

"Rock Around the Clock," said one girl. "Why Do Fools Fall in Love," hollered out another one.

"I'll play both of them but first, 'Why Do Fools Fall In Love'." Some kids were dancing — others were just sitting around chatting, and some playing checkers or chess. Still others were in line buying ice cream. You could buy ice cream on a stick or an ice cream sandwich. The sandwich was a square of chocolate, vanilla, and strawberry, nestled in between two slices of the same stuff ice cream cones are made.

The afternoon passed quickly and by Tuesday afternoon all books and rooms were pretty much ready for summer. There was always one exception to the rule and that was Miss Iris's room. She was a collector. There were always costumes, lights, books, papers, boxes, and junk of all sorts. The custodians always complained about her room. The final day of school would be Wednesday. Kids would pretty much have a free day. The elementary grades had picnics. The older kids were in class signing the school annual called the Torch. The graduation ceremony would start at two o'clock. It was held in the gym and not the auditorium because Mr. Hotchkiss and Mr. Dobronski would invite all the kids from fourth grade up to attend. The younger kids looked forward to seeing the graduation because in time they would be one of the graduates. The principals knew attending the graduation instilled school pride and love for their school. Along with the Roosevelt and Martin Awards, kids received their S pins which stood for Salina. The S pins were bronze, silver, and gold. During the three years in junior high school, students were allotted points for activities they were involved. The chess club, the Red Cross Club, sports, band, AVI, office assistant, and other extra-curricular activities. The parents and graduates would sit in chairs on the gym floor. There were three balconies for the student body. Teachers, special guests, and school leaders were up on the stage. It would be the highlight of the school year and everyone anxiously waited to see who would win the Martin and Roosevelt Awards.

"Good morning students," said Mr. Hotchkiss on the school intercom. "I have great news for you today. Today, is the last day of school and all of you will begin your summer vacation. Remember that we learn by everything we do. Please remember to be responsible young people. Help your parents around your home. Many of you have vegetable gardens and I hope you will do your share to weed and water the plants. Certainly there will be lots of swimming, baseball, picnics, basketball, and traveling. It has been a great school year; just as wonderful as it has been during all the years I have been your principal. It is my sincere wish that the summer months will be full of fun and pleasure and a mixture of responsibility. On behalf of all your teachers, all of the adults who help to make school enjoyable here, your parents, and our whole school community, have a great summer and play safe."

Mrs. Renko looked up at her class as Mr. Hotchkiss' ended his message. "There are many reasons why we have such a great school boys and girls. Mr. Hotchkiss, who just spoke those wonderful words on the intercom, is certainly one of them. You know boys and girls, Mr. Hotchkiss has been the only principal of this school since it opened its doors in 1918. He will be retiring in a few years but the legacy he will leave behind is measured in the success of many of the students who have sat in the same chairs you are sitting now. One of America's great artists is among them. His name was Zubel Kachadorian. I have a school annual that is several years old. You know it as the "Torch" that all of you are now sharing kind words and thoughts in the margins. The artist I was speaking about did the cover page for that old "Torch" I have. So be grateful because you have a wonderful principal who has shaped our school to be what it is." The students nodded in agreement and the looks on their faces demonstrated how much they liked their principal.

The day passed quickly and there were smiles and tears all around. Especially among the ninth graders that would be leaving and moving on to high school. They were going on to Fordson High School, one of the most beautiful high schools in America and the first to cost more than a million dollars to construct in 1928. Students began making their way down to the gym for the graduation ceremony. Parents began arriving and eighth grade students were handing out programs and seating them. The chairs on the floor were set back about 25 feet from the stage. There was an aisle down the middle and one on each side. The band was seated in front of the stage and the choir risers were up on the stage behind where the guest speakers and dignitaries would sit.

When all the parents were seated, and the students took their places in the balconies the graduation ceremony began. Jeff Durbin and John Calveri would handle the spot lights as the graduates entered the gym coming down the main aisle. The house lights were shut off and the spot lights would follow each graduate as they came walking in and the band played the popular Pomp and Circumstance Number One. This music was first played at Yale University and became part of graduations all over America from then on. Jeff and John did marvelous jobs as Mrs. Renko and Mr. Randall led the graduates. The spot light followed the teachers to where the graduates would sit. Each teacher stood one to the left and one to the right as the grads were seated. When all were seated, Mr. Dobronski came out to the podium and microphone.

"Good afternoon Salina graduating classes of 1955, parents, students, and honored guests. Mrs. Renko and Mr. Randall, would you please come up and take your place on the stage." There was thunderous clapping by the students and the graduates stood up as their homeroom teachers made their way to the stage. "Ladies and gentleman and students, we are honored today to celebrate the graduation and moving forward to high school these wonderful girls and boys. They are a great group and all of us here at Salina are very proud of each and every one. We know, graduates, that you will make us proud of your achievements in high school and hope you will come back and visit us now and again. At this time, I would like to introduce our principal, Mr. Hotchkiss." Again, there was applause and whistles throughout the gymnasium.

"Thank you Mr. Dobronski, and thank you boys and girls and all of our parents attending today's ceremony. Let me add to Mr. Dobronski's remarks how proud I am of both classes and how wonderful it has been to see most of you grow up and go through school here at Salina from kindergarten through your ninth grade year. I know you will be very happy and you will do well as you continue your education in high school. We expect great things from you. I have several honored guests today and I would like to introduce them to you. From our district court, the honorable Judge Martin, who will give out the Martin Award, named in his honor, to one of our outstanding students. Also, we have with us today, a former graduate and our city's police chief, Mr. Sam Jaffarr, who will give out the Roosevelt Award. Thanks to Mr. Faes, our band director, and Mrs. Leisenring, one of our choir directors. Weren't the songs and music terrific?" The audience again showed their appreciation though applause and whistles. "Our student council representative ninth grader, Rochelle May, will give out the Key to Success to one of the representatives of the eighth grade.

She presented the Key of Success to eighth grader Sally Hamood. The Key was passed to each succeeding ninth grade class. It symbolized the importance of working hard and striving to do well. The inscription on the Key read, "One has achieved success that has lived long, loved much, and laughed often. In doing so they have strived to help their

The Martin Award.

The Roosevelt Award.

fellow man, and conduct their life with honor and integrity." Mr. Hotchkiss was big on integrity.

After the students came up on stage to receive certificates of promotion, S pins, and other acknowledgements, Mr. Hotchkiss introduced Police Chief Jaffar, who would present the Roosevelt Award. The students waited in anticipation to find out who won the award. It was kept top secret. "For their outstanding scholastic and academic achievement, Carmella Costa and James Begian, come and receive the Roosevelt Award. The winners were so happy. Carmella had tears streaming down her cheek. Judge Martin awarded the Martin Award. He always repeated the names of the previous winners as he worked his way to the 1955 recipient. "I am honored to present the 1955 Martin

Award to Lee Turfe for his scholarship, attitude, and leadership."

As Lee, Carmella, and James stood on the stage they received a standing ovation. Lee smiled, and waved to the audience and Carmella and James waved and smiled, too. Each would take the trophies home for the summer and their names would be inscribed on them. The next year other students would be honored.

Mr. Dobronski came to the microphone and congratulated the kids, thanked everyone for being a great audience, and reminded the graduates and eighth graders about the Sunset Dance to be held in the cafeteria that evening. The art club spent the day decorating the cafeteria. Parents and students supplied different food dishes, deserts and drinks. Mr. Hotchkiss and Mr. Dobronski chipped in and ordered pizza from Joe's Pizzeria.

That evening the weather was just perfect. It was June, skies were blue, and the temperature was in the high 70's. The kids started arriving. Most kids could walk to the school and some got rides from their parents. The gang stopped in at Sophie's to chat before the dance.

"Pat, I love your dress," said Lynn.

"Your dress is very pretty, too, Lynn," chimed back Pat. "I bet we are a going to have a great time at the dance gang," Pat continued. "Who's going to look cooler tonight, the boys or the girls," she quipped.

"Come on, of course the boys are going to be cooler," said Neemer, as he nonchalantly straightened his tie.

"Our girls are beautiful and the coolest chicks in town," said Alan. "But I will tell you guys what is going to be the coolest thing happening tonight, Pat and Lynn. It was going to be a surprise but I think it would be alright to tell you now — especially you, Pat. Mr. Faes is going to have the dance band perform a few numbers and a few weeks ago he asked us four if we would sing 'Sh-Boom' as a present to the ninth grade class. You know we are hams. But we are good! We have been practicing with Mr. Faes and we think we are ready. No, I know we are ready. But I want to ask one thing. Pat, you and Junior are great dancers. When we get started with the song, we want you and Junior to come to the middle of the floor and start dancing the half-time. What do say, Pat? Junior already said he would." The Half-Time was the 50's version of the Jitter-bug.

"Of course I will. It will be a blast," she said.

"Great," Alan said. "Then as we get going we'll get the whole cafeteria rockin' 'n' rollin' and dancing to Sha-Boom!"

Sunset dances were part of the history of Salina. All during the 30's and 40's and 50's there were regular Sunset Dances held. One or both principals would be there and teachers would also chaperone. Parents

Dancing cheek to cheek at the Sunset dance.

Dancers having fun and smiling for the camera.

Make this a slow one please!

would also be there since it was a special night for the graduates. The kids started eating right away as the food looked scrumptious. While the band played, the kids were dancing to the tunes.

Mr. Faes got on the microphone and told the kids there would be a 15 minute break and a big surprise would be in store for them.

When Mr. Faes got back to the microphone, he called for everyone's attention.

"Students and parents,

Sha-Boom a hit by Crew Cuts.

teachers and all, we have a big surprise for you as four of your classmates are going to perform one of the biggest hits in America, 'Sha-Boom.' They have been practicing it for a couple weeks with the dance band and

I know you will all be delighted. So…house lights down…spotlights center stage as we hear the boys perform for your enjoyment and fun."

The boys all wore the same clothes. They had red plaid shirts, white slacks, and brown loafers. They parted their hair and it made them look older than they were — much like college kids looked.

The kids gathered around the stage clapping and yelling. Some of the girls giggled and Dino and his gang yelled out a couple swear words.

"1, 2 — 1,2,3,4 shouted Mr. Faes to the band and the boys began with "Sha-boom Sha-boom."

Everyone started clapping and soon, Junior and Pat were out there doing the half-time — the whole gym was dancing and rocking and rolling. There were two spotlights-one on the boys and one on the dancers. When the song was over, the kids were jumping for joy, yelling out the boys names and shouting congratulations of one sort or another. Mr. Faes went over and shook hands with the boys and had them and Junior and Pat take a bow. He told them how great a job they had done.

Later, he went to the microphone again and said to the audience, "Boys and girls, parents and teachers, we have come to the end of the graduation sunset dance and the band will play the last song. The ninth grade students selected the song "Graduation Day." While the band played, the kids could hear the song playing and they were singing and humming, "We'll remember always, Graduation Day!"

Gene and Beaulah stayed open late so the kids could come by and unwind from the dance. The store was jam packed.

"Gimme' a Sweet Sixteen Rock 'n' Rye and a bag of chips," yelled Bugsey.

"Hold your horses," said Gene. "Can't you see I am waiting on, Tommy!"

The gang found a table and they sat down to plan for the rest of the week.

"OK," said Alan. "Tomorrow we head to Camp Dearborn with the safeties. Friday, we meet and fine tune the raft and make sure we have everything."

"What time do we board the bus," asked Phil.

"Mr. Beckman said to be there at 7:45 am and the bus would leave at 8:00 o'clock sharp," said Pat.

Dreamy eyed Lynn asked, "I wonder if Clark Gable will be our bus driver again this year."

"He does look like Clark Gable. He is really handsome and nice. We'll see tomorrow," said Pat.

It would be a great day of fun at Camp Dearborn. All the safeties from the whole city would be there and enjoy baseball, boating, lunch, prizes, and all the pop, ice cream, hot dogs, and chips they could eat. It was a beautiful camp with a giant beach. There were beach umbrellas, a first-aid station, two different boating lakes, lots of hills, a canteen with loads of tables and chairs to hang out, a fishing lake, and a hill the older kids with cars called Roller Coaster Hill. It was a steep hill with a quick up and over dip much like a roller coaster ride — but in a car.

The bus was there waiting for the kids to arrive. It was parked at the corner just where the boys sit on the bars and watch the bustling activity in the neighborhood. There were 35 students boarding and all were there on time. Except for one!

"It is Clark Gable. It is Clark Gable," shouted Lynn to Pat as she got on the bus.

"Hi, Mr. Gable," chimed the girls. "You're so dreamy." The driver smiled at them and said thanks for the complement. The driver was a "dead ringer" for the great actor, Clark Gable. He looked over at Mr. Beckman and asked if all had come and should he take off. The kids heard him and together shouted, "No, Mr. Beckman, Alan isn't here. You know he is always late." Everyone broke out laughing. Just then Alan turned from the alley by his house and Mr. Beckman told the driver to leave as soon as he gets on. Alan had two shiny big red apples for the driver and Mr. Beckman. Smart guy!

Camp Dearborn was about 40 miles away and the driver would take Grand River all the way. It was one of the nicest and most popular roads in Michigan. It ran through many cities including Detroit, Old Redford, Farmington, Novi, and New Hudson. It was quite a scenic and rural drive passing through Farmington as there were farms and hills all along on both sides of the roads. For the gang it was a treat because they lived in the big city where factories, and stores, and busy streets were bustling all the time. There were silos, corrals, cows and horses, and fields of corn and wheat planted for end of summer harvest. Once through New Hudson, they turned on General Motors Road which was high on a hill. The kids could see down in the camp. The beach umbrellas were out already and boaters and swimmers were busy having a good time.

As they got off the bus and started looking for a picnic table to put their stuff, Lynn said, "Good thing we brought our bathing suits, the temperature is going to be 82 degrees and sunny all day."

"Wonderful," said Phil. "That means swimming, row boats, kayaks, and paddle boats, too."

"Whew," said Pat. "Take it easy. I want to hang out at the beach and get a tan."

"Here's a table to leave our stuff," yelled Alan. "It's close to the beach and to the bath houses where we can change into our bathing suits when we go swimming."

It was a fun filled day. Full of exciting games played between kids from all the schools attending. Lots of boating action took place. Everyone ate as much ice cream, soda pop, chips and hot dogs they could possibly eat. The park was very full with many people from all over the area. At the beach, the gang had a great time.

There was a first aid cabin right on the beach and trained lifeguards and medical people were on hand.

"Last one in the water is a rotten egg," yelled Phil. They scurried quickly across the hot sand and into the water. Everyone was an able swimmer. They learned in school and there was a neighborhood community pool they all enjoyed while growing up. There was a long three sided boardwalk that extended into the water. About ten feet

The beach at Camp Dearborn.

from the board walk was a lifeguard station where a guard sat and watched all the kids.

After swimming for an hour or so, the gang went up to the Canteen to sit and eat French fries and drink cokes, listen to the music, and dance on the tennis court next to the Canteen. Lynn and Pat decided to dance because none of the guys were in the mood. The girls were awfully pretty and in their bathing suits looked really beautiful. While they were dancing, the fellows looked over and saw a scuffle near where the girls were. A couple of guys were bothering them and the girls appeared upset. As the guys approached Lynn and Pat, one of the guys grabbed Pat by her arm. All of a sudden, "bam," "pow," "bam," Phil punched one in the nose, and Charles punched the other square on the jaw. They were strangers and not part of the festivities that day.

"Did you not hear them when they told you to leave?" shouted Alan very angrily. There were two other guys with them and Alan looked at them, and said, "Do you want some of what your buddies got? You don't get to put your hands on them! We protect the girls from our neighborhood punk. Get out of here before we really get mad and beat the living daylights out of you — all of you." They ran like the "dickens." Why naturally!

"You guys are the best. Thank you for helping us once again," said Pat.

"You know the code of honor we have from our neighborhood. We look out for each other. It's our duty," said Alan.

"Of course it is," said Charles. "Why naturally," they all chimed in. They all started laughing as they walked back to the beach area. Salina Wildcats do it again!

On the PA system the kids from all the schools were summoned back to the bus area. It was nearing time to board and get back to Dearborn. The leaders of the picnic gathered all the kids together. Soon they began drawing names for prizes. The many prizes included baseball gloves, bats, balls, tennis racquets, cameras, passes to local movie theatres, and more. But the grand prize would be awarded on the bus as each school boarded and readied for home. By four o'clock the kids were boarded and Mr. Stolls, from Triple A, who sponsored the outing, got on the Salina bus. He was quite a nice fellow with a big smile.

"Boys and girls," began Mr. Stolls, "I want to take this opportunity to say thank you for all the hard work you have done all year long crossing the children in your school each morning, noon, and after school each day. We are proud of how you performed on rainy days as you would wear the yellow Triple A raincoats to protect yourselves from the rain. Your diligence during the cold and snowy days we had the past winter is very much appreciated. It isn't easy to be out there every day in the cold and snow. Best of all, we can report that your school has continued its streak of no children hurt or injured crossing the many streets in your neighborhood. For 24 straight years your safety patrol has done a bang up job. Thank you also, Mr. Beckman, for being their teacher leader." The bus exploded with cheers for Mr. B.

"Now I know you have been waiting all day for the final drawing. One of you will win a brand new bicycle. So, driver, will you reach in and select the winner of this year's bicycle?" Just before he did, Mr.

Stolls took the box with all the names and shook it up, down, sideways and every which way. The Clark Gable look-alike bus driver reached in the box and took a slip of paper with one of the kids' name on it.

"And the winner is, Denise," shouted out Mr. Stolls. The kids began clapping and cheering for her. Denise was one of the hardest working safeties on the whole safety patrol. She was very happy as she hugged Mr. Stolls.

"The bicycle will be delivered at the school in the morning at the main office where you can pick it up, Denise. Congratulations to you. Thank all of you boys and girls for a job well done this year."

The end of year school activities were coming to a close. The kids sat back, tired, tanned, and ready to doze off as the driver pulled out on to General Motors Road to make the long trek back to the school. The gang was thinking about one thing: Rafting the River Rouge all the way to Greenfield Village and the Henry Ford Museum. Big things awaited them. So they thought!

The ride home on the bus was so quiet one could have heard a pin drop. Denise was beaming because she won the bike. Pat complained she had gotten too much sun. Norman was quite happy because he won a beautiful camera. The rest of the bus was pretty much laid back and sleeping right in their seats while Leonard passed around the baseball glove he had won. Tommy won a transistor radio. They hadn't realized the bus was just minutes from the school. The bus driver looked up into the mirror over his head that allowed him to see the whole bus.

"O.K., boys and girls, we are just about back to the school where I picked you up. The time is 6:30 P.M. and you have a couple of hours of daylight to grab your stuff and make it on home. Thank you for being courteous to and from Camp Dearborn. I hope I get this run next year at your school."

Just then Ronny shouted out, "Let's have three cheers for Clark Gable, our bus driver."

"Hip, hip, hooray. Hip, hip, hooray. Hip, hip, hooray," chanted the whole bus.

"I can see him smiling through the mirror," said Pat, as she nudged Lynn, her seat partner. "He's so dreamy. Remember when Judy Garland sang the song, "Dear Mr. Gable, in one of her movies? Oh, he is so, so, dreamy!"

When they were all off the bus, the gang gathered at Gene's store for a quick meeting to discuss the final plans for the trip down the Rouge.

"Hi Gene and Beaulah," shouted the gang as they entered the store. We just got back from the Camp. They quickly ordered drinks and sat down at the round table to talk.

"Listen, everyone," said Charles. We have to decide when we are leaving, how long it will take, our final course, and all that."

"Yeah," said Al. "We have to check the weather to be sure it will not be raining or a severe storm. Gene always knows the weather. Let's ask him."

"Hey Gene, could you come over here a minute, we have something to ask you because we know you are an expert," said Neemer.

Gene walked over and asked, "What is it kids?"

"Gene, you always know the weather forecast and we are wondering what it will be like the next few days," one of them said.

Gene took out the Detroit Times weather page and put it on the table. With his hand, he skimmed down to the report. The kids saw that he had a missing finger tip and couldn't help but remember the day someone asked how he lost it. He told us that one day he was so hungry, he ate it. Everyone broke out laughing. Oh, well! He continued, "Friday, tomorrow, will be sunny and a beautiful day. But Saturday evening and Sunday it calls for rain and storms. The rest of the week will be very nice and pleasant. I also heard the report on my short wave radio this morning."

"Thanks, Gene," they answered.

"O.K. everyone, listen," said Charles. "Tomorrow we will go put the final touches on the raft. We'll get it ready and leave early Monday morning. How does that sound?"

"Sounds like a winner," they all agreed.

"Hey, everyone," said Phil. "Neemer and I were going to go shoe shining to make some money so we could buy snacks and stuff for the trip. Can you finish the raft without us," he asked.

"Of course we can," they all said.

"We can do it all man, we can do it all," said Alan.

"O.K., that's a plan. Friday, you guys make some money for the trip and we'll finish the raft. Saturday, we'll go to the show to see….."

"To see what?" they hollered.

"Rock Around the Clock, with Bill Haley and his Comets," replied Charles. "Frank, the theater owner finally ordered it."

"Man, it will be great, we'll be dancin' in the aisles," said Lynn.

"One o'clock, two o'clock, three o'clock, rock," they sang out in Rock and Roll fashion.

The next morning the gang met again at Gene's. School was over but the teachers were still in the building finalizing records and making sure their rooms were ready for summer cleaning before they left for the summer. With Gene's being directly across the street from the school, the kids could see the hustle and bustle of teachers and adults coming and going. The rope for the big flag pole was pulled up to the second floor window. They saw Denise and her mom as they loaded up the bike into her mom's car.

"Finish your doughnut and drink everyone. It is time to get over to Baby Creek and put the final touches on the raft," said Charles.

"I got enough canvas from Shakar's Tarp and Tent," said Dr. Bones. "He gave it to me free of charge. He said we could cut the grass this summer for him and that would settle the account."

"Great. The Patton Park ranger was nice enough to give us the logs from the poplar trees they cut down. They were perfect size being about 12 feet long," said Charles.

"What about the inner tubes that Acme Trucking gave us," Alan said. "My cousin, Jimmy Ferris, works there and his boss said we could have them. Jimmy patched the holes in them and they're as good as

The gang adds the inner tubes by tying them to logs. Planks would be added for floor.

new," he continued.

"Excellent," said Charles. "When we tie them under the raft, we'll be able to slide the raft down the hill right to Baby Creek. It works perfect for us. Otherwise it would be too heavy to move."

The gang went to work on the raft, getting the canvass sail ready, tying the oars on to both sides. The plan was to take turns paddling when the wind was not useful for them. During this time, Phil and Neemer met at the UAW local union hall where they would start shining shoes. Those fellows were nice dressers, liked their shoes shined regularly, and were great tippers. They were the union officials representing the Ford Rouge Plant workers.

"I got enough black polish to get us through the guys at the local," said Neemer. He continued, "We will stop at the Popular Corners Drug Store and get a new tin of Kiwi Polish from Wally or Bert. Then we'll head down Vernor all the way to Skid Row. Maybe we'll have to use that blue liquid polish you brought that shines any color shoe," he added.

Vernor Highway connected the neighborhood with downtown Detroit. Walking along Vernor, heading east, would be General George S. Patton Park on the left and Woodmere Cemetery on the right. Hidden Lake was in the Woodmere Cemetary. This area was referred to as Southwest Detroit. It was the most populated area per square mile than any Detroit neighborhood because much of the car industry was located in Southwest Detroit. There was the Fleetwood Plant on Fort Street that made the Cadillac. There was the Cadillac Plant on Clark Street between Vernor and Michigan Avenue. There was a Chrysler Plant located at McGraw and Wyoming. Together, with the Rouge Plant, they employed 300,000 people. There was lots of hustle and bustle — lots of stores and lots of bars. Hardworking men going and coming to work in the factories would eat and drink at the bars. Neemer and Phil would concentrate on the bars. It was a perfect setting. They would walk in and approach each patron sitting on a high stool and say, "Care for a shine sir, just 15 cents." The men enjoyed getting their shoes shined while enjoying a cold brew of ale. Sometimes they got four or five shines in a bar. It was hard work shining shoes. One had to be careful not to get polish on the patron's sock.

As they criss-crossed Vernor Highway, going into one bar after another, they would pass many large stores. There was an A & P, Federal Department Store, many shoe stores, drug stores, coney island restaurants, the Rio Theater, and ever so much more. This was before they got to the Michigan Central Train Station. The train station took passengers all over the Midwest to New York. It was a beautiful 15 story building, with lots of marble floors, and murals painted on the walls. The boys had been working more than three hours when they reached the train station. Outside was a gentleman with his baggage enjoying the warm day and reading the newspaper as he sat on a bench.

"Care for a shine sir, only 15 cents," said the boys together.

"Boys, as you can see my shoes are a cream color and I am certain that you don't have a color for them." Just as he finished saying that Phil got his attention.

"Sir, not a problem. We have a special polish my brother brought home while he was in the Air Force."

"Really?"

"Really!" said Neemer. "The Air Force doesn't lie."

"Ok, then, go ahead and shine 'em up," said the man.

The polish was a liquid blue and the directions stated to sprinkle on the shoe and start buffing. Phil began the sprinkling while Neemer watched. While the man set his foot on the shoe shine box,

The shoeshine box with polish and a place on top for the customer to place his foot.

he sat back in the bench, and continued reading the newspaper. The more they buffed and sprinkled the more the shoe started to turn blue. The boys began to panic as they knew something was wrong. They quietly packed everything back into the shoe shine box while the man continued to read. As they took off running, the man put his newspaper in his lap and looked down at his one cream colored shoe and one blue shoe. The man was furious.

"What did you do to my shoes you little brats," he screamed. "Let me get my hands on you."

He began chasing them down Michigan Avenue where Vernor connected. He quit chasing after a block or so tired, huffing, and puffing, and realizing his suitcase was left unattended. The boys saw that he quit as he turned around heading back. Neemer hollered to him. The man turned around and looked.

"Hey sir, that shine is on us. No charge." They continued down Michigan Avenue. Just as they were walking along the sidewalk next to Briggs Stadium, the home of the Detroit Tigers, two big ugly scraggily fellows stopped right in front of them.

"You boys got 50 cents? We need some money," said the meanest looking one.

"What did you say," said Phil.

In an angry tone and with his eyes widening and popping out of his face, he repeated, "I said you two punky kids got 50 cents?"

The boys were really scared and what was worse, they had already made more than 30 dollars. They knew these bad guys were going to take all of their money. Phil and Neemer had to act fast so they flung a couple of kicks and grabbed the shoe shine box and ran across Michigan Avenue once again. The crooks didn't follow. A police car had driven by and those fellows disappeared behind the stadium. Saved by the cops!

The stadium meant a lot to the gang. They came to many Sunday double headers — especially when the Yankees were in town. They would buy bleacher seats way out in deep center field for 75 cents and climb a fence to get into general admission seats. When they saw seats not being used they would sneak even closer to the Tiger dugout often ending in the box seats. The box seats along third base were the best seats in the stadium. The kids were to the city what Huck Finn and Tom Sawyer were to the Mississippi River. They were daring and always taking a chance. The kids in the Bronx and Brooklyn, in New York, had nothing on the South Enders!

The Tigers were one of the oldest teams in the Major Leagues. Ty Cobb played for the Tigers and is considered one of greatest players of all time. Hank Greenberg, another Tiger, hit 58 homeruns and almost broke Babe Ruth's record of 60 homers. But their favorite player was

Al Kaline. Kaline joined the Tigers when just 18 years old and soon won the batting crown. Everyone in Detroit loved him. When the gang played baseball on the playground and one of them would come up to bat, they would imitate and act out the batting stance of Kaline and call out, "Here he is ladies and gentleman, coming to bat is Al Kaline — the Kid! That was how Van Patrick, the voice of the Tigers would say it. That is how the boys did it every time, "Al Kaline, the Kid." So cool!

The shoe shine boys reached "Skid Row." It was two blocks long, with one bar after another. An hour or two would make them even more money. The bars were so close to each other it was as though one would walk out one door and the very next door is another bar with a bunch of guys hanging and drinking. No matter so long as they wanted their shoes shined. The last bar was just a block short of Bagley Avenue where the boys would take the Bagley bus to Vernor and be home before dark. They counted their money and it totaled a bit more than 42 dollars. It was a lot of money for two boys to earn. They shined a lot of shoes! Why naturally!

The rest of the gang had finished up with the raft. They were able to keep it in the park ranger's yard. It was quite a raft. There were several logs that were tied together with very strong rope. The giant truck inner tubes were attached to the bottom of the logs. Wooden planks were nailed to form a deck on top of the logs. It was Dr. Bones's idea for the inner tubes. He thought it would give the raft enough buoyancy to make the trip. Two large oars were attached also to not only row but guide the raft as they made their way down the Rouge River. The canvas was put on a roller much like a window shade and could be rolled down when it was not needed. It was quite a raft. The gang only hoped that it would float like they planned and get them where they wanted to go. The plan was to meet at Tripepi's that evening to finalize their adventure on the River Rouge. It would be the first Friday night of their summer vacation and Saturday was movie day at the Fordson Theater. Time to Rock and Roll!

The gang arrived at seven that Friday evening at the store. Neemer was busy playing the football game where the steel ball is kicked up by turning a handle that controls the kicker; it maneuvers through a maze of prongs where the person playing tries to catch it. The ball is then returned for a free kick. This was a game of skill. He was tough to beat. Lynn was playing the rifle air game where the balls would bounce inside and fall into the curved areas. She did pretty well. Charles called the group to order as they sat at the counter. Part of the group sat on the long bench that was just opposite from the stools. This way they could face each other.

"Let's give Neemer and Phil a round of applause for working so hard and being generous to share the money they made today shining shoes," said Charles. "With that money, we can get some baloney and salami, bread, chips, and whatever to eat while we are sailing. They almost got robbed, you know."

"Yeah," said Phil. "We stopped at Chimes for a hamburger deluxe and after we turned some poor guy's shoe blue at the train station, we began running toward the stadium. These guys came out of nowhere. They wanted to separate us from all the money we made."

"No way were we going to let them do that!" said Neem. "So when I heard Phil tell them the money was in his back pocket, I knew something was going to happen because I had the money. He put his hand in his pocket as though he was getting the money and then hauled off and kicked one of the guys. The guy yelled in agony. Just then, boom! I kicked other guy in the leg and we took off like we running for a touchdown. It was a close call."

"While you guys were busy doing that we completed the raft and it is ready to go."

"I have an idea. Rather than make it an overnight trip so we don't have to lie to our parents, let's leave early and get back before dark. What do you think?" said Pat.

"I like that idea, too," said Alan.

"Me, too, me, too," chimed a chorus of the whole gang.

"That settles it. We are a democracy and the people have spoken," said Charles. "We'll meet early and tell our parents we are going to catch frogs and tadpoles at Lapeer Pond and have a picnic. That's just a little white lie. They don't count."

The plan was all set. The gang stuck around for a bit, played the juke box and the games and left for home. Saturday would be Rock and Roll time at the show.

The Fordson Show in the gang's neighborhood was a bargain. It cost only 12 cents to get in. Candy bars were a nickel. So was a bag of chips. The fountain coke was a dime and it was enough for two to share. The marquis was lit up by hundreds of yellow light bulbs. It always said the following: "Selected Pictures–Always a Good Show."

The neighborhood was so diverse that often movies of different languages were shown on slow nights for the adults' entertainment in their native language. The ticket booth was right at the sidewalk and doors to enter were on the left and right of the ticket booth. Going into the lobby on the right was the confectionary that sold all the goodies the candy boy would bring in to sell in the theater. The candy boy wore a beige type jacket and carried a box that had straps that went around his shoulders. The box stood right in front of him as he walked. The box was really large and could hold several cokes, candy bars, boxes of pop corn, Holloway suckers, and much more. While watching the

The Fordson Show marquis adds a special feature — "Rock Around the Clock."

movie, the candy boy would walk up and down the aisle and the kids would yell out to him to get his attention. "Candy boy, send me a Milky Way."

Rock Around the Clock, the movie that Saturday, proved that Rock 'n' Roll was the music of the young people of America and the Salina neighborhood, too. Bill Haley was one of the pioneers of Rock 'n' Roll and the movie was about how it happened. Alan Freed, a popular disc jockey and promoter of Rock 'n' Roll was in the movie, as well. Even though it was about the struggle rock stars faced the kids were only interested in the "beat," the music, and the dancing and singing.

The girls would go in groups and so did the guys so the show was a place for romance, too. The boys would parade around going up and down the aisles hoping that one of the girls would let him sit next to her and watch the movie. Sometimes you would see older kids, "making out" but most of the time the boy would only put his arm around her shoulder. The ushers were always telling the kids to find a seat.

The gang sat down to enjoy the movie. "Candy boy, let me have a box of Milk Duds, or a box of pop corn, or some Juju Beads," could be heard.

"Hey candy boy, bring me a bag chips and coke," yelled Bugsey, one of their friends. "Watch this," he said to the gang. "I got this slug which is exactly the size of a quarter and coated it with some silver paint to make it look like a quarter." The candy boy came over and gave him the coke and chips and Bugsey handed him the slug and said, "Don't forget my change." Sure enough, the candy boy gave him back a dime. They all cracked up laughing.

The world news appeared on the screen first and then the cartoons. Finally, the movie began. "One o'clock, two o'clock, three o'clock... rock, four o'clock, five o'clock, six o'clock, rock...gonna' rock around the clock tonight..."

There it was on the big screen. Bill Haley and His Comets were singing the hottest song in the country. The show went wild. Everybody started dancing and singing. They were in the aisles, jumping in their seats, singing and clapping. Junior and Pat were great dancers. Not only could they do the half-time, but they were great jitter bug dancers, too. The crowd hollered, "We want Pat, we want Junior!" They hollered over and over. The candy boy put his candy box down and he was rockin' 'n' rollin', too. Someone grabbed the spotlight that was attached near the stage and focused it on Pat and Junior. Soon they were on the stage doing the dandiest jitterbug in Dearborn. The kids gathered around the stage watching them, singing, and clapping. There they were in front of the movie on the big screen where Bill Haley and his Comets were playing and there was Pat and Junior. From the back of the theatre, it looked like they were in the movie, too. What a day. What a movie! What great dancers Pat and Junior were as everyone clapped when they came down from the stage. They had to. Frank, the manager, was screaming and hollering and pulling out his hair; except he had no hair! Oops!

When the movie was over, they met at the Popular Corner Drug Store for a coke. This store had a long counter and it was a very prosperous business as it was right on Dix Avenue. The Ford Workers would come on their breaks for snacks and drinks. They sold most everything there. The owners, Wally and Bert, were great guys!

"Let's meet at the middle stairs where we play Three Flies Up after dinner and make our final plans. What do you guys think?" said Charles. Everyone agreed. They would meet at the school and set the time for their trip.

Everyone showed up on time and they began with the final plan to leave for the adventure of their lives. What the gang did not know was just what the adventure would really entail. Science fiction was about to take its place in Dearborn, Michigan, in 1955. What a ride it would be! Of course, what do you think!!!?

With the raft built, the gang made ready to bid bon voyage to their neighborhood. They met at Baby Creek. The plan was to embark from Baby Creek, sail to the Hidden Lake, and from there sail on to the River Rouge. The raft was full of snacks, games like checkers, chess, and battleship. One of the girls brought her camera to capture sights. But the most important gadget aboard was Dr. Bones's gadget invention he called — The Time Machine. He called it that because he said they could go back in time and travel forward again. So he said!

"You don't think that contraption is going to work, do you?" asked Neemer.

"Of course it is," he replied. Everyone started laughing and joking. He made it from an old radio but it was what was inside that he claimed would boggle their minds.

"Just you wait, we are going back in time and it will be amazing!" The gang laughed again uproariously. "We'll see who gets the last laugh. I will! When we get to Fordson Island near where the British built the warships used in the American Revolution and the War of 1812, I plan to take us back in time." He said it with an eerie laugh and smirking look on his face while rubbing his hands together. They laughed again!

Baby Creek had quite a history. One of the very first settlers in the Salina area, back to the early 1700's, was a man named Baubee. His farm had more than 1000 acres and Baby Creek sat right in the middle of it. The farm became a municipal park where people would picnic, go swimming, play baseball, handball, and tennis. On hot summer afternoons, moms would bring their younger children to swim and wade. The creek was about the size of a football field. The deeper portion was roped off for safety. The creek ran south under Vernor Highway and straight to Hidden Lake inside Woodmere Cemetery. As the years passed, what was once named Baubee Creek — became Baby Creek.

Hidden Lake was nestled inside the cemetery very close to Riverside Street which formed the city boundary. The cemetery was one of the oldest cemeteries in Michigan and had a crematorium. Many Civil War veterans were buried at Woodmere. When they studied the Civil War, Mr. DeKay, their social studies teacher, took them on a field trip to study the graves and the history of the Civil War. There is much to learn about history by studying grave markers. There was a huge statue

Hidden Lake in the cemetery would lead the gang to the Rouge River and Fordson Island.

of a Union soldier standing guard over his fellow union soldiers who fought bravely in the Civil War. The lake was quite deep. Weeping willow trees and other kinds of trees formed the perimeter of Hidden Lake. Kids from the big city would steal bikes and bring them to the lake and submerge them to hide the bikes from the police and a few days later come back and get them. Sea gulls and geese gathered there in large numbers. Once the gang tried to swim there but right away came a cemetery worker who chased them off. They knew they had to be careful not to be seen when their journey began.

From Hidden Lake, the raft would sail south toward the River Rouge. It would pass Fordson Island, and the Fairlane Mansion and on to Greenfield Village and the Henry Ford Museum. Fordson Island was on the Rouge which flowed to the Detroit River where the gang would dock for lunch. It was going to be quite a trip. They estimated the journey to take several hours before reaching the Village. They planned to sneak into the Village. The gang planned to hide the raft and tour the Village and then sneak into the Museum. The museum was once referred to as the Edison Institute Museum. In October of 1929, the museum was dedicated to Thomas Edison and every person that was anybody in America — and the world — was there for the dedication. It was called, "Lights Golden Jubilee," in honor of the light bulb's 50th anniversary. Dr. Bones could not wait until they got to Fordson Island. He had a plan. It was a plan that would shake American history. So he said!

The gang secured everything to the raft, slid it down the hill toward Baby Creek. It was early morning as the sun had just come up. They looked east toward downtown Detroit where the sun began to climb over the tall buildings. They looked at each other. Then Alan spoke, "Do you guys remember Mr. Ewasek? He was that substitute teacher and later became assistant coach to Mr. Costea. That week he subbed he taught us several foreign words and their definitions? Do you recall any foreign words that are appropriate for what we are about to challenge?"

"I remember one," said Pat. "I really liked it, too. It was the Latin/French word — derive. It meant a spontaneous journey where the travelers leave their life behind for a time to let the spirit of the landscape, nature, and architecture attract and move them. I have a feeling that might happen to us as we travel the Rouge."

"There was the German word, sturmfrei. It means the freedom of not being watched by a parent or superior, being alone at a place and having the ability to do what you want and succeed," added Charles. "It seems that is just what we are about to do. There will be no one to watch us, nor anyone to tell us to do this or that. It will be just us — on our own."

"I like the one that describes what we are about to do best of all. The Latin word numinous describes experiences that make you fearful yet fascinated, awed, yet attracted — the powerful, personal feeling of being overwhelmed and inspired," said Phil. "So here we are and here we go!"

"I remember the word Yugen, a Japanese word. It means an awareness of the universe that triggers emotional responses too deep and mysterious for words," said Dr. Bones. I promise you a ride

through the universe that will mystify you when we go back in time."
He smiled that smirky smile and rubbed his hands together and put
the Time Travel Machine on the raft. Oy Vey!

Soon the gang stopped at Fordson Island, which was on the Rouge
within a quarter mile of the Detroit River to the south, and very close
to where the Rouge Plant was a bit to the north. The French established
a shipyard along the Rouge right where Fordson Island was in the early
1700's. They built small boats called batteux and canoes made of bark
some of which were 40 feet long.

In the French and Indian War, the French lost the shipyard to the
British. Beginning in 1760, the British began major renovations and
made the shipyard much larger. These ships were to patrol the Great
Lakes and became the biggest shipyard on the Great Lakes. The British
were to use the shipyard all through the American Revolution and up
to the War of 1812.

When the gang docked their raft to stretch their legs and have
lunch, Dr. Bones brought his Time Machine along. They sat along the
shore of the Rouge to eat and have something to drink.

Fordson Island where Dr. Bones takes out his invention, The Time Macine.

"Oh, I see Dr. Bones you brought your little Time Machine to lunch with you," said Neemer in a sardonic way.

"I sure did!" said Dr. Bones. "Not only that, after lunch we are going to go back in time. The gang all looked at each other and then looked at him and started laughing, too.

"Mr. DeKay told us how the British took over the French shipyard that was right smack dab here!" said the Doctor. "Isn't that right?"

"That's right," said Pat. "He told us the troop ships built here were to go down the Detroit River and attack Fort Detroit."

"I remember now," Alan added. "General Hull, the commander of the fort, was fearful that the British along with the Indians, led by Chief Tecumseh, would wipe out the fort including all the women and children. Add to that, the general's family was in the fort, too."

Pat added, "The general did indeed surrender the fort. He was later arrested and convicted of cowardice and about to face a firing squad. But President Madison nixed that because General Hull was a hero during the American Revolution."

"You guys got the picture correct and Mr. DeKay went a bit further with the story. He told us that a year later, in 1813, we took back the fort from the British," remarked the crafty Dr. Bones.

"So," said the gang in unison.

A typical fort similar to Fort Detroit in 1813.

With that smug grin and smile that Dr. Bones was famous, he told them that they would be going back to the year 1813 and would be helping the American soldiers and sailors get the fort back.

"No way," said Alan.

"Impossible," said Charles.

"Are you nutty?" they all rang out.

"No way? Impossible? Nutty? Well, are all of you done eating? Are you guys ready to go back in time? Do you want to take an hour or two and give it to those British who stole our fort? Because I am! We will give the British a taste of their own medicine — Salina Wildcat style," he told them. They all looked at each other and shrugged their shoulders, tilted their heads, and stared at one another.

"Tell us, Mr. Dr. Bones, just how did you create this box that looks like a radio, a bit like a miniature television, wires leading hither and there, this antenna that goes up and down into the machine, and this strap to hold it," asked Pat.

At that point, all of them leaned in close while they completed eating their lunch to listen how he built his Time Machine.

"Well, I studied general relativity that Einstein talked about that included the fundamentals of curvature of space and time. These wires represent that idea. Then I read what Newton's Law of physics implied that space and time are absolute. So with those two thoughts in mind, I started thinking I can create a device that extracts energy from curved space and time which would create a concentrated field of closed time linked curves for time rate control and power generation," replied Dr. Bones. "I invented this Pliblaster Glow Tube that would deliver the energy for us to roller coaster ride through space and time," and he began laughing. "When I place it inside the Time Machine, we are good to go." Dr. Bones inserted the Pliblaster Tube and smiled at everyone.

"So from all that you are telling us," said Pat, by turning this dial to a certain year back in time like 1813 (she turns the dial), then turning this other dial to the on position (she turns the dial) and then pressing this button…"

The moment Pat pressed the button it was like the finale of the fireworks on Fourth of July. The explosions of colors and shapes and the sounds of boom, boom reverberated. The gang became quaquaversal (moving

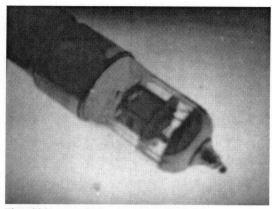

The pliblaster tube invented by Dr. Bones.

in every direction in the air instantaneously). Their ride through time became a wild and whimsical journey in a state of unpredictability. Going through their minds as they turned and tossed and floated about were fear and anxiety and anticipation — all jangled together. Yet, the gang was fascinated and awed by what was happening to them. They thought how strange and unfamiliar these moments were but could not help feeling it was marvelous.

Suddenly they all landed upright and safe. They looked at each other. They really looked at each other! Their clothes had changed in some magical way. They were wearing pants with breeches that came to their knees just like in the colonial days. Their shoes were made of leather and in the style of the colonial period. The girls were dressed the same and one could not tell who was a boy or who was a girl except — the girls had pretty faces, of course. Each had colonial style hats and right where they stood were seven ponies — one for each of them. The ponies would prove to be very important to the gang.

"See, I told you. I told you we were going back in time because I am an inventor. I am the famous Dr. Bones." As he pranced about triumphantly he shouted, "Now do you believe me?"

They all shook their heads in agreement with complete shock on their faces.

"Don't worry gang," Dr. Bones said. "We will do what we planned to do and that is help get our fort back from the British and teach them a lesson they will never forget. He put his right hand up in the air pointing with his pointer finger and prancing and telling them they were about to change history — Salina Wildcat style. Why naturally!

"You know what is really funny," said Charles. "We are actually in our own neighborhood but at a time more than a hundred and forty years ago."

"Gotta' hand it to you, Dr. Bones," said Neemer. "I was getting on your back and laughing at you. I am not laughing anymore! But tell me — tell us, can you get us back to our own time?"

Dr. Bones looked at him, and then looked at each of the others. They all stared at each other in wonderment and leaned their heads to listen.

"Of course, I will get us back. As soon as we get our job done here, we should be on our way," he said with that smirky eerie kind of laugh and rubbing his hands together very briskly. "Lookout you British!"

The whole gang knew how to ride horses. They would go over to the Imoberstag Farm off of Brady Street and do chores and Mr. Imoberstag would let them ride horses. Riding toward Fort Detroit would be no problem. They could see the town from where they were. The trip through space made them hungry so they decided to go find something to eat. They jumped on their ponies and off they went to the little town on the Detroit River.

The town they saw from a distance had twelve houses, a church, a little school, a bakery, a carpenter ship, a livery stable, and several other small structures. There was one very well built building that was guarded by several British soldiers. The actual fort was a mile down river but the well built building was the commanding headquarters where the British made their plans to attack Americans ships and towns along the Great Lakes. People were free to walk to and fro so long as they didn't stir up trouble. The War of 1812 was on and the ships they were building played a major part for the British to control the Great Lakes.

Galloping along the way the gang could see some commotion in the distance. As they got closer, they could see a bunch of teenage kids taunting a group of Huron Indians. The Hurons were teenagers, too. When they stopped, they could hear the words being spoken to them.

"You people are nothing but a bunch of dirty redskins. You can't come through our town and go shopping in the general store," said one of the bullies.

"Your town?" asked one of the Hurons. "This is our land and you have stolen it from us. It is our town more than yours," said the tall handsome Huron Indian boy. "Just because there are just a few us and many of you, it does not give you the right to mess with us or put your hands on my sister and scare my little brother." Their parents were the British soldiers and sailors that commanded the fort and the area.

The gang looked over as the Huron pointed to his sister. The Indian boy looked at the gang on their ponies and explained all she wanted to do was purchase some seeds and other supplies and get a peppermint stick for the little brother to take back to their village. He said inside the store one of them starting bothering her and taunting her because she was so pretty.

"We got here just in time before one of them hurt my sister," said the Indian boy.

"Pat and Lynn, stay on your horses. Fellows let's go settle this problem in a fair way. It seems that even back in time during the colonial period there are bullies," said Charles.

"We're not staying on our ponies," said Pat. "We know how to fight if we have to."

"That will be enough of bothering the girl and the little boy, and that remark about dirty redskins doesn't sit well with me," said Alan.

"It doesn't sit well with any of us," chimed the gang.

"I suggest you go about your business and leave well enough alone," said Phil.

"This is none of your concern. Who are you, anyway," said the big mouth in their group, just as he grabbed hold of the Indian girl.

With that, her brother grabbed him and told him to let her go.

The others jumped the Indian boy and the gang jumped all over him and them. Fists were flying, bodies were being tossed, and dust was everywhere. The gang took care of business and soon the bullies were off and running. The girls held their own in the skirmish, too. The Salina Wildcat girls knew how to fight, too!

"Thanks," said the older brother. "These guys always make trouble for us when we come to town. They act tough when they out number us but not when we have a group in equal number."

"I know, it is like that where we come from, too," said Charles.

"Where do you come from? We have not seen you before," said the pretty Indian girl.

"That's a long story," Pat said. "It is much too long to explain today. Maybe the next time we come we'll tell you all about it," she said.

"Won't you come to our village and join us for something to eat and drink?" the tall Indian boy asked.

"We would love to come and visit your village but we have some important business to take care of," said Dr. Bones with the smile he made famous. "We promise that you will know much more about us very soon. We plan to make a little noise and you might hear it back in your village. Is your village close to that big hill over there in the distance?" asked Dr. Bones.

"It sure is. We can see the whole town and all the boats along the pier from on top of the hill," said the big brother.

"Good," said Dr. Bones. "Watch for us in an hour from up there and I think you will be pleasantly surprised."

The Indians mounted their ponies and promised to watch for them and off they went waving back at the gang after thanking them again. The gang waved good-bye, also.

"She sure was beautiful," said Alan.

"She sure was," said the rest of the boys.

"Take it easy fellows, take it easy, we've got business to take care of," said Lynn.

"Lynn is right. But the next time we come back, we'll invite them to visit the future," said Dr. Bones laughing and rubbing his hands together.

The gang had made its way back in time to 1813 and right away they show their spirit of doing the right thing by standing up for the Huron Indian teenagers. CRD would be proud of them. So would Mr. DeKay. The objective was to help return Fort Detroit back to the Americans after General Hull had surrendered it to the British in 1812. President Madison would be sending William Henry Harrison, who was later to be elected president, to recapture the fort. It would not be easy but it had to be done. The British had been too powerful with their ships on the Great Lakes.

The gang snuck into the mess hall of the British naval command and found fresh bread, toasted cakes, cheese, jam, and lots of fresh cider to drink. The gang ate quickly and headed to the command headquarters to find out the British plan to fight Commander Oliver Hazard Perry, sent by the President Madison to help General Harrison capture the fort. The British knew that Commander Perry was on his way because he had just defeated them in the Battle of Lake Erie. But the British were ready — or so they thought.

The gang was eves-dropping from outside the window of the British command office.

"We have just received word that we lost the Battle of Lake Erie to the Americans," said their General Ashcroft.

"Hooray," shouted Lynn.

"Shush, do you want them to catch us?" said Alan.

"Oops, sorry," she said.

"It seems they have this upstart, Commander Oliver Hazard Perry, commanding them aboard a frigate called the Lawrence. It is heavy with cannon. We must stop them or lose Fort Detroit back to the Americans," said the commander.

"Sir, we will be ready for them," said one of his officers. "We have the 154 ton, General Gage ship, built right here at the Rouge shipyard. It can carry a crew of 45 with sixteen four-pound cannons."

"Sir...Sir...," said another officer, "I command the Rebecca, a 136 ton brig, 37 men, with fourteen carronades and many swivel cannons."

The British were well prepared to meet the Lawrence. There were several other smaller boats including the Angelica, the Faith, and the Adventure. It was going to be quite a battle on the Detroit River. All of these boats and more had been built at the Rouge Shipyard. All of them were docked right at the Rouge River and Detroit River juncture. The ships were battle ready and only needed to up anchor and meet the Lawrence as it approached Fort Detroit.

"O.K. then, let us thrash these brash Americans and give them a lesson they will not forget! Do you know what this Commander Perry said when they won the Battle of Lake Erie?" The British soldiers shook their heads no. 'We have met the enemy and they are ours,' that's what he said. Now let us go out into the Detroit River and make him realize the enemy is still here to keep control of this river and the Great Lakes. God save the King," the commander shouted.

"God save the king," they all shouted, as they rose and hoisted their drinks to the British flag.

"Did you hear that," said Alan.

"God save the King," said Neemer. "The heck with the king — we're Americans we don't believe in kings and queens!"

"Teach those Americans a lesson," said Lynn. "The nerve of those British to say that!"

"These guys are in for a big surprise. We will teach them a lesson they will never forget," said Phil.

"So what is the plan," asked Pat. "How are we going to stop all those ships from attacking the Lawrence," she continued.

"Don't forget," said Charles, "General Harrison is following the Lawrence in troop transport boats to retake the fort when they land. If all those boats go out to meet them, they will easily sink the troop transport boats with all the American sailors and soldiers."

Again, the gang looked at Dr. Bones. He was the brains of this idea of helping the American soldiers and sailors recapture Fort Detroit.

With deep stares and eye to eye, they looked at their pal for leadership and the plan.

"Dr. Bones has a plan," said Dr. Bones.

"Well, what is it for crying out loud," they all seemed to shout.

"It is simple. Well… not that simple. Well… it is complex. Well not that complex," he said.

"What?" they all shouted.

"We are going to blow all the British boats up and sink them right in the harbor," said the Dr. "All except for the big one because it is anchored out too far from us. Their biggest boat, the General Gage is out about 200 yards. It is too far for us to get to. It will have to be handled by Commander Perry. If we sink or damage all the other ships, I know that the Lawrence will win over the General Gage."

Now the gang was even more bewildered. All they ever knew back home in 1955 time was playing basketball, going camping, dances, hanging out at Gene's and Tripepi's, and having fun. How in the world were they going to BLOW up boats!

"Dr. Bones, oh, Dr. Bones, are you with us?" asked Pat. He was in deep thought. She snapped her fingers much like a magician brings someone out of a trance. He shook his head as though he was awakened.

"Of course, I am with you. I am the famous Dr. Bones. How many times do I have to tell you guys?"

"Then tell us!" they all pleaded.

"Here's the plan. I brought along blasting caps I found at the Clippert Brick Yard and Quarry on the other side of Tractor Park. They use them to set off dynamite to break up the slag and stone to make brick. So I stuck them inside the Time Machine and here they are."

"Did you bring the dynamite, too?" asked Alan sarcastically.

"No, but I brought a timer and a remote and enough wicks to set off the explosions," he said.

"But no dynamite, right?" they asked.

"We don't need dynamite," said he. "Each of the boats has lots of -barrels of gun powder on them. They use the gun powder to fire the cannon. Only this time, we will use the gun powder to blow up the rest of the gun powder barrels which will sink and damage the boats. We are going to sneak on board each boat, set the wicks, and put a blasting cap which we will be able to ignite by pressing the remote. You get it now?

"I get it," said Charles.

"We all get it," said the gang.

"But isn't it dangerous? Maybe we will blow ourselves up, too!" said Lynn.

Dr. Bones walked over to Lynn and got eye to eye with her and bending his head and said, "Blow ourselves up? This is the great Dr. Bones. I have covered all angles. You see, I left the remote back with the Time Machine. Only the remote can ignite the blasting caps. I suspect that they will eventually see us and wonder what a bunch of kids are up to."

"Oh, I get it," said Charles. "We set the wicks, timers, and the blasting caps near the gun powder in each of the ships and then we high tail out of there on the ponies."

"He's getting smarter all the time," said Neemer.

"Here is the clincher," said Dr. Bones. "We will all get back safe and

The ships docked around the British headquarters on the Detroit River.

sound all accounted for and then let the music begin!"

The gang tied up their ponies near the dock and started strolling along the boardwalk where the boats were docked. They blended in with all the other British kids walking about. The plan was to casually walk up and down while two of the gang would sneak aboard each boat and plant the wicks and the blasting caps. It worked like a charm. The girls got the attention of the guards by asking questions about England and how long they have been at this fort. The British soldiers watching did not have a clue.

Just as they finished the very last boat, the Angelica, the call to board the boats and meet the Americans was being spread throughout the shipyard. Several of the British sailors came just as the gang finished. They approached the gang and asked them who and what were they doing in a restricted area.

"We came to watch the fireworks," hollered out Neemer laughing heartily.

"There are no fireworks here. Who are you?"

"We're the Salina Wildcats you ninny," said Pat.

British soldiers hanging around the compound in 1813.

After that remark, the leader of the British sailors told his men to grab them and take them to command headquarters to see General Ashcroft.

"O.K. you kids let's go," said one of the British sailors.

"Do you mind if we ride our ponies over there sir," said Phil.

The leader allowed them to get on their ponies and they began to take them to headquarters. Or so they thought.

"Are you ready gang? Let's get back to where the Time Machine is. We are about to head forward in time right back to Fordson Island," said Doctor Bones. "1955 here we come!"

The sailors were caught by surprise as the gang went into full gallop — the other way. The British were on foot and chased after them but the gang was way ahead of them.

When they arrived back to where the Time Machine was, Dr. Bones got a little bold with the pursuing British.

"An hour ago your commander quoted Commander Perry after he defeated you at Lake Erie. Well here is another message for him. Tell him that a group of Salina Wildcats of Dearborn, who came from the future, have a message for your commander."

The gang got into position as Dr. Bones had told them. He also told them just as he finishes talking to the British he would push the button that would take them back to 1955 and Fordson Island.

"Tell your commander that Commander Perry will soon be here to sink the General Gage deep into the Detroit River," said Dr. Bones. "Tell him also that General Harrison will soon follow and take back Fort Detroit. Finally, tell him this, just as Commander Perry said, we now say, too. The Salina Wildcats have met the enemy and they are ours."

Just as he said, "…they are ours," Dr. Bones pressed the button on the remote. All of a sudden the sounds of bombs louder than any thunder began. One ship after the other began to "blow." The blasting caps worked. The barrels of gun powder began to explode. The gang could see the first ship begin to sink in the harbor. Then the second one

Plumes of smoke rise from the boats after Dr. Bones hit the remote to ignite the blasting caps.

sank. The other ships were ablaze with fire and smoke and lit up the sky. The British sailors began running from the ships. The soldiers chasing them could see it also. They turned and looked at the gang. They began coming right to them to capture them and bring them in.

The ships, one after the other, begin to go up in smoke.

The gang accomplished their goal to help win back Fort Detroit.

The gang was in complete awe. They had just blown up five of the British navy ships that were going to go out to meet and challenge the Lawrence captained by Commander Oliver Hazard Perry. They were in complete disbelief. Suddenly they began cheering and jumping around.

"There is no time for cheering; it is time to get ready to go forward in time back to Fordson Island. Are you ready? Here goes," said Dr. Bones. He set the dial to 1955, turned the switch to on, and pushed the button.

Immediately the gang was flying again through the air just as they did when they went back in time only this time in reverse. The experience was similar but different. It was kind of like

The Time Machine.

clockwise versus counter clockwise. Suddenly, once again, they were back on Fordson Island. Gone were the ponies and the clothes. But still with them was the knowledge of what they had accomplished. The navy battle was a success. Commander Perry did sink the General Gage and General Harrison and his men took back the fort. The American flag once again was flying high on the pole. Salina Wildcat style! Why naturally!

The gang was never to realize how happy the Indian teens were. But when the Hurons heard one of the boys say there would be fireworks that evening, the Indian teens watched from upon a hill nearby cheering for them. They saw the chase and watched as the boats went afire and exploded shooting flames high into the sky. The Indian girl asked her brother if he thought they would ever see them again. "Something tells me that could very well happen," he told his sister.

They all boarded the raft and began their journey on the Rouge toward Greenfield Village and the Henry Ford Museum. Charles and Phil manned the steering and set the sail. The others were tired from the excitement and fell asleep.

Commander Perry leads his men into naval battle on the Detroit River to recapture Fort Detroit.

"Wake up all you guys. We are passing Henry Ford's Fairlane estate," said the guys. They had gone under Michigan Avenue. Michigan Avenue heading west went all the way to Chicago.

"What a beautiful house," said Lynn. The river is going right through the forest of trees, flowers, wild bushes, and lots of wild animals running free in the heart of a city."

"Mr. Ford was one of the richest men in the world. It is no wonder the Fairlane Mansion is so beautiful," said Alan. "They have tours of the mansion. Maybe this summer we'll come back and visit it."

"Greenfield Village is just about 20 minutes from here. We'll beach the raft behind the old Smiths Creek railway center where nobody will see us," said Charles. "There are so many wonderful sights to see in the Village. Mrs. Woodbeck, my fourth grade teacher, brought us here on a field trip. I sure did love her," he added. "I will never forget seeing the chair President Lincoln was sitting in when John Wilkes Booth shot him. It is kept in the Logan County Court House where President Lincoln practiced law. I hope we find time to visit the courthouse," Charles concluded.

"We are going back in time once more before we head for home," announced Dr. Bones.

"Uh, oh," they all said.

"Have no worries, Dr. Bones is here. Didn't I tell you we would change history? Didn't I? Didn't I? Didn't..."

"Yes, yes, yes," they all hollered back.

"So what's the plan," asked Alan.

The plan was to go back to

The chair President Lincoln was sitting when John Wilkes Booth shot him at Ford Theatre.

Logan County Court House where President Lincoln practiced law.

October 21, 1929, and watch famous people from all over the world pay tribute to Thomas Edison. On that night, Dr. Bones explained to them, Henry Ford planned a celebration called, "Light's Golden Jubilee Dinner." It was the fiftieth anniversary of the incandescent electric light that Thomas Edison invented. It also was the night that the museum was dedicated to him. Henry Ford admired Thomas Edison very much and wanted to honor him.

"We'll discuss it later as we tour the Village because we are here," Dr. Bones replied.

There was a perfect spot to beach the raft out of the sight of the visitors on that day in 1955. Summer vacation had started in schools across the nation and the Village was one of the favorite places to come. People from every state and most countries, if not all, came to see the many fine historical buildings brought from other states and countries and rebuilt exactly as they had been.

"We are looking at about three o'clock in the afternoon," Pat said.

The inside of the courthouse. Notice the cabinet in the back of the room. It was made by President Lincoln's father.

"We have to shove off from here by seven or so in order to make it back before nightfall. All agreed?"

The gang nodded in agreement and they set the visiting agenda. They would visit the Sir John Bennet Jewelry Building from England that had Gog and Magog, full characters, who chime the bell when the clock struck at the half hour and the hour. The glass shop was a must to watch as skilled glass blowers blow into twenty feet long blow tubes while the mixture at the end of the tube was held in fired 1200 degree ovens. Out would come beautiful works of glass of all shapes by blowing in the tube. They would visit the Town Hall where plays and musicals would be performed. That particular day the gang would see a tribute to George Gershwin, the great composer of the 1920's and 1930's. The Noah Webster House was brought to the Village to honor the man who created the Webster dictionary. They would visit Henry Ford's birthplace and home, the Wright Brothers Cycle Shop, Stephen Foster's home, the Logan County Courthouse where Lincoln practiced law, and several other exciting historical locations. It took a full day to get through the whole Village but the gang didn't have that much time.

The plan was to go back in time — so said — Dr. Bones.

The gang was nearing the end of the visit when they stopped to get a frozen custard near the Sir John Bennett Building.

While they sat there the clock struck five o'clock. Out came Gog and Magog. "Clang" they hit the bell once, then twice, then three times and four, and the last clang was five o'clock. The crowd enjoyed watching it — especially the children. The chime could be heard throughout the Village. One of the gang asked why the clock hands were off and the village attendant told them a craftsman from England was coming to repair it.

"It's twilight zone time again," said Dr. Bones. "You guys ready?"

They all looked at him. Then they all looked at each other and shrugged their shoulders in agreement.

"Lynn, you set the dials this time. Pat did the honors at Fordson Island," Dr. Bones directed.

She turned the dial to October 21, 1929, Dearborn, Michigan. It would be one of the greatest nights in the history of America. The most famous scientists, artists, writers, inventors, doctors, architects, and more had come to Dearborn, Michigan to honor Thomas Alva Edison in the "Light's Golden Jubilee Dinner." The museum would be named in honor of Mr. Edison.

Sir John Bennett Building brought from England to Greenfield Village.

"O.K. everyone are you ready? All I have to do is push the button," she said.

When she pushed it, the gang once again felt the tumultuous

boom, boom of sounds like thunder. The colors were like a prism of rainbows — only these weren't the normal rainbow colors — they were violet, yellow, red, blue, chartreuse, green, and orange. They were in a state of numinous (feeling of being awed, fearful, attracted, and inspired) fascination while their bodies were catapulted in a quaquaversal manner. When they came to rest, they were still in front of the Sir John Bennet Building with a sense of unfamiliarity, rareness, strangeness, but feeling marvelous. The people were wearing different clothing. They noticed a fellow riding a bicycle with a front wheel as tall as six or seven feet and a rear wheel a normal

Bust of Thomas Edison on display in Salina School Library.

bicycle size. Their clothes were different, too. The girls were dressed in beautiful evening gowns. Their hair fixed ever so lovely. The boys were wearing black tuxedos with patent leather shoes and derby hats. What a change from the colonial days! And what do you know? There was a lovely horse and carriage waiting right there. The driver assuming they were going to the dinner at the museum said, "May I take you to the museum? I am sure your parents are there waiting for you."

"He thinks we were invited to the dinner," whispered Pat.

"We were," said Neemer. "We invited ourselves. May I help you to your seat on the carriage, Miss Winona," said Neemer as he extended his arm. Winona is a Native American name that meant princess. Pat was her nickname. Her family came from Oklahoma to Dearborn. She had a lot of Native American blood. She meant business when they fought the British. "Hooray, Winona!"

"Miss Lynn, may I help you, too?" asked Alan.

The horse and carriage that took the gang to join the "Jubilee."

Then in a jingly chant we heard:

"Dr. Bones has done it again. Dr. Bones has done again." There he was — Dr. Bones chanting and dancing and jumping up on the carriage. He hid his Time Machine in the bushes between the Town Hall and the frozen custard stand — close to Gog and Magog. "Hey Gog and Magog, watch over the Time Machine for me. We'll be back in an hour or two," and he started belly laughing. "Let's go dance with destiny," he said. "Driver, to the museum — thank you very much."

"Did he just talk to the statues up in the clock?" someone asked.

When they arrived in the front of the museum in the carriage, the porter greeted them at the start of the red carpet. As they stood in front of the museum, built as a replica of Independence Hall in Philadelphia, they watched as famous men and women from all over the world got out of Model T and Model A Fords.

They were dressed in evening gowns of white and black and men with formal tuxedos and derbies. Some even had top hats. There were military men dressed in a multitude of colors serving as honor guards and attaches.

Events that day saw President Hoover and Thomas Edison arrive at Smith's Creek Station. This was the station that Mr. Edison worked as a young man and Henry Ford brought and rebuilt in Greenfield Village. As a youngster, Edison sold newspapers there and served as a telegraph operator. Many of the guests went to the Clinton Inn and enjoyed lunch. Mr. Edison grew tired after lunch and went back to the Fairlane Mansion for a nap.

That afternoon, at his Menlo Park laboratory, now in Greenfield Village, Mr. Edison, along with Henry Ford and President Hoover, reenacted the moment Thomas Edison successfully created the incandescent light. He sat down in his chair while the president and Henry Ford watched. It was reported live, coast to coast, by NBC radio commentator, Grahame Greene:

"Mr. Edison has two wires in his hand; now he is reaching up to the old lamp; now he is making the connection. It lights! Light's Golden Jubilee has come to a triumphant climax!"

Picture of Gog and Magog, the bell ringers.

Museum entrance to the "Jubilee" dinner and festivities.

Thomas Edison reenacts the famous moment when the first incandescent light became part of history.

The laboratory was jammed full of onlookers, reporters, and guests for the evening. They clapped in thunderation when the light lit up. It was like going back in time. Know what I mean?

It was evening when the gang entered the main part of the museum. The museum was elegant. Beautiful drapes hung above the very large windows. There was an enormous and absolutely gorgeous chandelier hanging in the middle of the dining hall. Another chandelier hung above the speaker's table where honored guests would sit. The American flag was hanging above the speaker's platform. There were gold ribbons running down the centre of each table. Beautiful and colorful flowers adorned each of the tables. The floor was made of imported teak laid in geometric angles.

When they entered, the usher said to them, "Right this way, young ladies and gentlemen. Mr. Ford has reserved this area for children of the guests."

"Could you tell me sir," said Neemer, "have my mom and dad, Mr.

The train arrives at Greenfield Village in 1929 as President Hoover and Henry Ford meet and greet people.

and Mrs. Eastman, arrived?"

"Are you referring to the founder of the Kodak Camera, young man?"

"Yes, of course," Neemer replied.

"I don't think so sir," he replied.

President Hoover and Henry Ford join Thomas Edison at his laboratory.

"Well, when you see them, be sure to tell them we are fine and seated, and promise to behave. We will see them back at the Dearborn Inn across the street."

"I shall do that."

What a night it was going to be. As the guests began to arrive, the gang was flabbergasted.

"Look, there are Will Rogers, Edsel Ford, and Walter Chrysler, coming in," said Lynn.

"I can't believe my eyes. It is Marie Curie, the great scientist coming in with Charles Mayo, the famous doctor and researcher," said Alan.

The gang was in awe. They saw Walter Briggs, Harvey Firestone, Fielding Yost, Albert Kahn, Ransome Olds, Orville Wright, John D. Rockefeller, and so many more. All together there were 500 guests. They were seated when they heard:

"Ladies and gentleman, the president of the United States, President Herbert Hoover and Mrs. Hoover," said the man on the loudspeaker. They were coming up the main aisle. As they entered, everyone rose to their feet and cheered. People reached out to shake hands with the president as he came up the aisle. Again, the man on the speaker said:

"Ladies and gentleman, Mr. Henry Ford and Mr. Thomas Edison are now entering." The people rose up again cheering and applauding. Soon they were seated at the front table with the president.

"Can any of you believe what we are seeing?" said Charles. What a night! The most influential people in America and throughout the world are here to pay tribute to one of the greatest inventors of all time," he continued.

"Dr. Bones, we owe it all to you. You are a great inventor, too," said Neemer. In an inquisitive and apprehensive manner he asked, "But tell me, are you sure you will get us back home?"

"Why naturally. Haven't I got us this far? Are you forgetting who I am?"

They all said in unison, "You are the famous inventor, Dr. Bones!"

Dr. Bones smiled with that characteristic smile, rubbed his hands together and said, "Riiight!"

Just then Mr. Ford heard their voices say the word inventor and looked over at them and stared for a long moment.

There was a special tribute via radio from Albert Einstein. Several speakers rose to the podium and spoke and so did Mr. Edison. Mr. Ford declined to speak so as not to take away any of the limelight of Thomas Edison.

"The experience makes me realize as never before that Americans are sentimental, and this crowning event of "Light's Golden Jubilee" fills me with gratitude. As to Henry Ford, words are inadequate to express my feelings. I can only say to you that in the fullest and richest meaning of the term — he is my friend. Good night," remarked Tom Edison.

"Wow, I got goose bumps all over," said Pat.

"I know," said Charles, "we are witnessing parts of America's greatest moments in time."

The gang could not help but notice throughout the evening that Mr. Ford kept looking over at them. They were getting a little nervous and wondering if their ruse was up. Nearing the end of the program Mr. Ford motioned to a fellow and whispered something to him. The next thing the gang knew there were four security people behind them.

"Mr. Ford wants to know who you kids are and what you are doing here?"

"Excuse me, Mr. Bennet," said the usher who escorted them, "this young man here, (points to Neemer) told me to relay a message to his parents, Mr. and Mrs. Eastman."

"Fine and dandy," said the security man, "but the Eastman's don't have any children do they young man?"

"Don't they?" asked Neemer. He scratches his head pretending to be perplexed and says, "I wonder how that happened."

"Let's go, all of you. Mr. Ford wants to talk to you in his private office."

The evening festivities had ended and the gang was led to an office upstairs near the front of the museum. They all looked at each other wondering what the next step was going to be. As they waited in the office, which the security man locked, they checked the windows and all the other doors and they were locked tight.

"All we have to do is just go back in time to escape," said one of the kids.

"Won't work that way," said Dr. Bones. "We must get back to where we were in front of the Sir John Bennett building. Remember when we were chased by the British. We had to get back to Fordson Island where we went back in time. That is the only way it will work," he said. "Somehow we must escape back to that point. We must come and go from the same spot. Plus, I hid the Time Machine behind some bushes there. Anyway, let's meet Henry Ford and tell him how much we like him and how we enjoyed the evening."

Just then, in came Mr. Ford and Thomas Edison.

"Just who do these kids think they are," said Mr. Ford shouting. "Disrupting the evening and being where they did not belong!"

"Now, now, Henry, youngsters will do mischievous things. You know that I always did and so did you. Let us hear what they have to say."

"Where are you kids from," said Mr. Ford.

"Dearborn, sir," they all replied.

"We were born and raised in the neighborhood by where the Rouge Plant is," said Phil.

"How did you get here?" he asked.

"On a raft we built," they chimed in. "We sailed the Rouge."

"Let's see you came on a raft, down the Rouge River, passed the Fairlane Mansion, and arrived at the Village?" asked Mr. Edison.

"Yes!" they all screamed. They told him they started from Fordson Island.

"In tuxedos and evening gowns, no less," said Mr. Edison.

"Well that's a long story sir," said Alan. "You see, we have this Time Machine and, er, well…you tell him Dr. Bones. You're the inventor."

"Inventor? My, oh my!" replied Henry Ford. Raising his hands in the air he shouts, "Now they are inventors, too. They crash into your party and now they tell us they are inventors, Thomas."

The gang went on to tell Mr. Ford and Mr. Edison all about their activities, their brush with the British, their trip down the Rouge, beaching the raft, and going back in time for the "Light's Golden Jubilee." They explained in detail about the Time Machine and the great inventor, Dr. Bones. Dr. Bones was smiling that smile the whole time. All of a sudden the great men bursted out laughing and dancing as though they were doing an Irish Jig. They loved to dance especially when they were camping with the group they called the Vagabounds. Famous men would join them as they camped across the country. They would often dance at the camp fire.

"Show us this Time Machine. Mr. Ford and I are always looking for new ideas and inventions," said Mr. Edison.

The gang agreed and told them where it was. Reluctantly, Mr. Ford ordered a large carriage to take them back to the Sir John Bennett Building where they hid the Time Machine behind some bushes.

When they arrived, Mr. Edison was most interested. He and Dr. Bones spent a bit of time going over the details of how he built it in the carriage. Mr. Ford was chuckling and telling Mr. Edison that it was just a gadget and the kids were hoaxing them. Still, Mr. Edison, always the inventor, was intrigued.

"You see Mr. Edison, as we said, we have been back in time once before," said Dr. Bones.

Both of the great gentleman listened as they told the story about blowing the ships at Fort Detroit and how that helped win back the fort. They told them about the whole plan and only the gang, Mr. Edison, and Mr. Ford knew about the Time Machine. They loved the story. But the look on Mr. Ford's face told them he wasn't buying the story. Mr. Ford told the kids he was proud of their being imaginative and even more proud that they were Dearborn kids like him. Mr. Edison wanted a demonstration even though he was not sure about the whole thing. They arrived back where they hid The Time Machine.

"Are you sure you want a demonstration?" asked Charles. "If we set the dials we would end up back in 1955 right here in front of Gog and Magog," he added. "Positive," said Mr. Ford.

"Absolutely," said Mr. Edison.

"Before we shove off, may we say how wonderful it has been to meet you both. We enjoyed the "Light's Golden Jubilee" so much. Meeting you and seeing all of those great people sure has been something great for all of us to remember," said Pat.

The gang shook hands with each of them. Pat and Lynn gave them hugs. The gang looked around to see everything as it was in 1929 and prepared to go into orbit once more. They all knew that Mr. Ford and Mr. Edison would be in a state of disbelief and that they would not see them again. They also knew the great men didn't believe them. Mr. Ford and Mr. Edison were in for the shock of their lives.

"O.K. sirs," said Dr. Bones. "All I have to do is set the dials to 1955, grab hold of the strap on the Time Machine, and push the button."

"Go right ahead," said Mr. Edison.

The kids all looked at each other, shrugged their shoulders, smiled at two of the greatest men of all time, and watched as Dr. Bones went to grab the strap on the Time Machine and push the button. Suddenly, Dr. Bones tripped and as he grabbed for the strap his other hand pushed the button by mistake. Zazoom…the gang was jet propelled once again. This time, the colors mixed and matched and crissed and crossed and their bodies were doing somersaults.

When they came to rest, gone were the evening clothes, gone were the horse and carriage, gone were Mr. Ford and Mr. Edison, and gone was the…Time Machine.

"Oh, no," said Dr. Bones, "when I slipped, I could not grasp the strap on the Time Machine very well. It must have slipped out of my hand. The Time Machine is back in 1929 with Mr. Ford and Mr. Edison. I must have grabbed the pliblaster glow tube by accident. Here it is in my hand. Without the pliblaster glow tube the Time Machine will not work," he added.

The gang looked about and here they were right in front of Gog and Magog and heard the clock strike eight. It was 1955 again. As they looked up, they watched the bell as Gog and Magog chimed eight times. They stared at each other and all of a sudden broke out with uproarious laughter. They had done it. They met Mr. Ford and Mr. Edison. They had done all they said they would do. Salina Wildcats do it again!

"You know gang, we can't raft back home now because it will be dark soon," said Charles.

"We can take the Michigan Avenue bus right back to Wyoming and then take the street car home," Alan said. "We'll be home before dark."

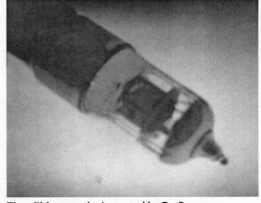

The pliblaster tube invented by Dr. Bones.

The gang agreed that would be the best thing to do so that their parents would not worry about them. They left the raft. So the gang walked down Oakwood, caught the bus on Michigan and were on the street car and back in the neighborhood while it was still daylight. They were tired. As they walked home, Dr. Bones started to laugh.

"Why are you laughing," the gang wanted to know

"It's really funny," he said. "By now, Mr. Edison is trying to figure out how the Time Machine works. Too bad! When my hand slipped and just as we began to orbit the pliblaster glow tube I created fell out and right into my hand. Mr. Edison will never know how the Time Machine worked."

The gang went home to sleep. It is said that in the Museum, down in the basement archives gathering dust, is a funny looking machine with a tag attached to it that read: "Mr. Ford and Mr. Edison's Time Machine that never worked. But both men insisted until the day they died they saw seven kids from Dearborn go into orbit and forward in time." So they said. Why naturally!

CPSIA information can be obtained
at www.ICGtesting.com
Printed in the USA
FFOW03n0831111017
40913FF